DUMB LIKE ME, OLIVIA POTTS

DUMB LIKE ME, OLIVIA POTTS

by Lila Perl

A YEARLING BOOK

Published by
Dell Publishing Co., Inc.
1 Dag Hammarskjold Plaza
New York, New York 10017

Yearling ® TM 913705, Dell Publishing Co., Inc.

ISBN: 0-440-42028-8

Reprinted by arrangement with The Seabury Press.
Printed in the United States of America
Third Dell Printing— April 1981

CW

DUMB LIKE ME, OLIVIA POTTS

1

I, Olivia Potts, was sitting upstairs in my room, leaning on the windowsill and watching red leaves, the color of dried blood, drop off the maple tree that grew just behind our house.

"Brains," I groaned softly to myself. "Brains, brains, *brains*!"

In front of me was the homework assignment that Miss Kilhenny had given our fifth-grade class that afternoon. The English homework was the worst. There was this list of words:

collaborate
obliterate
eject
phenomenon
reminisce

"Now," Miss Kilhenny had said, turning her head of tightly waved, battleship-gray hair toward the window side of the room so that her steel-rims caught the glare of the hazy blue October sky, "I want you all to put each of these words into a sentence, an *intelligent* sentence, one that will tell us the *meaning* of the word, one that *uses* the word in such a way that another word *cannot* easily be used in its place." She looked around. "*Do* you all read me?"

Heads bobbed all over the room and voices murmured, "Yes, Miss Kilhenny."

Possibly I'd nodded my head too readily or said yes too loudly. Or maybe it was doomed to happen anyway. Miss Kilhenny's eye fell on me and suddenly I felt as though I'd swallowed a whole fish—a small fish, but alive and slippery and squirming hard inside me.

Miss Kilhenny's upper lip stretched across her teeth, the closest I'd ever seen her come to a smile. "As for you, Olivia, I'm going to ask you to do a special assignment because I know that English is a strong point in your family and I want you to work in this class to the full measure of your potential."

I could feel the twenty-six pairs of eyes of the other kids in the classroom on me. We'd been in Miss Kilhenny's fifth grade for nearly a month now, but this was the first time she'd singled me out in front of everybody.

"Don't feel I've singled you out, Olivia," she continued. I gulped. Besides being cranky, fussy, stuffy, and terrifically strict, was Miss K. a mind reader as well? "As I learn more about the rest of you," she went on, "you'll all be required to work up to your full potential in given areas."

Her gaze shot back to me. "What I want *you* to do, Olivia, is to use these five words in a one-page story or essay, rather than in five separate sentences. You may fill in with additional sentences if you have to, and you may use the past tenses of the verbs. You'll get extra credit, of course. But I warn you, the story must make sense. We'll be watching for that, won't we, class?"

"Yes, Miss Kilhenny."

"Oh, and one more thing, Olivia. You will add a *sixth* word to your list." She turned to the blackboard, drew a line under the five words that the whole class had been assigned, and beneath it wrote her extra word for me. The word was: *potential*.

Now, at nearly half-past four in the afternoon, I hadn't even done my math homework yet. Outside my window, even though there wasn't much of a breeze blowing, the dry red leaves seemed to be giving up all on their own. You could almost hear them sigh, "Why struggle?" and drop gracefully to the lawn below. Even as I watched, chinks were opening up in the tree, which had been a solid mass of green all

3

summer. Some of the spaces were big enough so I could see through to the back gardens and driveways and garages of the houses on the street in back of us and just around the corner from us.

In one of the houses around the corner, new people had been moving in all afternoon. Now the moving men were sitting at the barbecue table in the backyard, drinking beer or soda and getting ready to leave. Over at the Delaney house, which was directly behind ours, I could see Norman Delaney and one of his friends—it looked like Harvey Epping—moving something around in the garden. It was a big cardboard crate and looked heavy. Finally they lugged it over toward the garage and I couldn't see them anymore. Norm and Harve were seventeen or eighteen. They had left high school about a year before and didn't hang around in the neighborhood much anymore.

I'd walked home from school that afternoon with Norman's eleven-year-old brother, Buzz, who was in my class. Buzz wasn't awfully bright. I'd heard he'd been left back in kindergarten! But he had a nice freckled smile and he always wore dark pants, not jeans, to school and even a shirt with a tie sometimes.

"Why's old Killer Henny after you, anyway?" Buzz wanted to know. "She got it in for you or something?"

"Oh, didn't you *know*?" I replied sourly. "Hadn't

4

you heard? I come from a very brainy family. My brother Greg just started in at Yale this fall. On a scholarship. And my sister Meredith won a city-wide high school poetry contest last May. She got *first* prize. A hundred dollars."

Buzz kicked at a stone, loosened his tie, and undid the top button of his shirt. It was one of his tie days. He was even wearing a navy-blue blazer with brass buttons. "Yeah, I heard about your brother. He was the big hero in the high school graduating class last spring."

I didn't mean for Buzz to think I was showing off. I remembered that his brother Norman had known Greg during the first few years of high school. But of course they'd never been close friends. Greg was the top and Norm, to put it bluntly, was the bottom.

"But what's all that got to do with you?" Buzz went on.

"What it's got to do with me," I explained, "is that Miss . . . that Killer Henny had both my sister and my brother in sixth grade. She remembers them well, and she feels responsible for bringing out the brain power in both of them. Now she's got me, the last of the litter, and she's not going to let me slip by without working me over a little. In fact, I'm surprised she took this long getting around to it. Get it?"

"Yeah," Buzz said thoughtfully. "That's rough on

you. And she isn't even a regular fifth-grade teacher."

It was true. Miss Kilhenny was a sixth-grade teacher and probably the oldest teacher in the school. Well, anyway, she'd been there even longer than the principal. We were supposed to have had Mrs. Lacey in fifth grade and I'd spent the whole summer lazily and happily looking forward to it. Mrs. Donna Lacey was about twenty-five and recently married. She was pink-cheeked and creamy-skinned, with light-brown hair that she wore piled high on her head. Silky little tendrils always escaped and curled around in front of her ears and at the back of her neck. I think I was even a little bit in love with her. All through fourth grade I'd been an office monitor, and even when I didn't have a message to take to her fifth-grade classroom I'd always managed to pass it in the corridor and peek in just to get a glimpse of her.

Then, on the very first day of school in September, Mrs. Warren, the principal, had walked in and told us how lucky we were that a fine sixth-grade teacher like Miss Kilhenny (who was now standing right beside her) had been willing to step in and take over in an emergency. The emergency was that Mrs. Lacey was expecting a baby and was having some problems that meant following doctors' orders and staying off her feet in the early months of pregnancy. We were lucky, too, Mrs. Warren said, that the sixth-grade registration was low enough this year so that they could consolidate five classes into four, freeing "this most distinguished member of our staff."

When I told Meredith and Gregory, who was packing his car with last-minute gear for the drive up to Yale, they were "happy" for me. I could have killed them both.

"It's only because you're disappointed about Lacey, on whom you obviously had a schoolchild crush," Meredith said with that calm, frosted, know-it-all air she had lately developed. "You'd probably have been assigned Kilhenny in sixth grade anyway. She's a hard-liner, of course, but so what? You don't want to go on being fed pap all your life, do you?"

Well, I don't know what you'd call the kinds of poems Meredith writes. Not pap, I guess. She writes poems like:

Into the gray and roiling
    corners
        of my mind,
crepuscular, murk-ridden,

Dark, bedeviled
    thoughts
        drift.

I ache.

So much for Meredith's poetry. I put Miss Kilhenny's list of words underneath my entire pile of school books and started on my math homework. Everything was quiet outside my window now. The car parked in the Delaney garage had finally backed out of the driveway and silently disappeared, and the moving men at the house around the corner had left their empty bottles on the barbecue table and roared away in their truck. Only the crumbly red leaves kept on softly drifting down.

Suddenly the front door downstairs opened and banged shut, and heels clattered across the hallway into the kitchen. It wasn't Meredith. She always wore sneakers, gum soles, earth shoes—things like that. It had to be my mother.

A few seconds later Mom came clattering up the stairs and was standing in the doorway of my room. Her dark, straight, short hair was mussed up, some of it sticking in her eyes, and her cheeks were flushed a deep red.

"Oh, Ollie," she puffed, "there you are." (Where did she expect me to be?)

She came in and flopped down on the corner of my bed, her legs slightly apart and her hands tossed limply between them in the hollow of her pleated skirt. She took a very deep breath.

"Somebody been chasing you?" I asked.

"Feels like it." Mom laughed. "Today's been such a

8

rush. And it's not over yet. Actually it's sort of just beginning." She leaned forward. "Ollie, they've accepted me. I'm registered and all. Me! Really."

I dropped my pencil on the desk and leaned back in my chair next to the window. I had an idea what she was talking about.

"You mean at college? Is that where you were this afternoon?"

"Right. Believe it or not, your mom is now enrolled at Eastborough Community College for an associate bachelor-of-arts degree. They took me. Even though I was late and classes began three weeks ago."

I smiled weakly. It seemed to mean a lot to her. There was this special "pilot program" of late-afternoon and early-evening classes for adults with high school diplomas. Mom had never been anything but . . . well, a mom. She'd never had a job, not even worked as a saleslady just before Christmas or a part-time checker at the supermarket. The most she'd ever done was write out bills and statements for some of Pop's regular gas-station customers and put them in envelopes and addressed them. She couldn't even type except with one finger.

When she'd first heard about the new "on to college" program for people living in our borough of New York City, she joked about it in a kind of "what if," half-serious way. Then she decided she was "too busy" getting Greg off to college and taking care of Meredith and me and Pop and the house. Then Greg left and she found she wasn't too busy after all, and Meredith really kept working on her. Pop was quiet about it but he did say that if Mom really wanted to "go off and get as educated and as brainy as her three children" it was okay by him.

So there it was. The classes at the college hadn't filled up because lots of grown-ups were hesitating like Mom was. And so they'd put a notice in the paper announcing that registration was being extended through the month of October.

"What are you going to be studying, anyway?" I asked.

"I'll be taking two courses this semester," Mom said. " 'Social Psychology' and 'The Family and the Community.' What do you think? It sounds challenging, doesn't it?" Already, she was beginning to sound just the littlest bit like Meredith.

Mom began kicking her legs up and down in front of her. There were slightly swollen threads of varicose veins on both of them. After all, Mom was forty. She said the veins came from having three children and putting on too much weight with each pregnancy. But she'd had a pretty neat figure for the last few years. Not ravishing, but neat. I guess in a way I looked a lot like her. Round face with straight, thin nose, short, straight brown hair, big round glasses

10

that made *me* look like an owl (Mom didn't wear glasses but Meredith did). And, like Mom, everything about me was medium—medium height, weight, looks, coloring. Nothing outstanding.

"I wonder," Mom said girlishly, "whether I should wear a skirt or pants when I go to classes. Maybe a skirt would be better the first time."

"When's that?" I asked idly.

Mom glanced at her watch and jumped up. "My heavens, it's in an hour! At six o'clock."

"You mean tonight?"

"Yes. I didn't realize it was getting so late. Merrie'll be home soon. And your father at seven." She looked worried. "I could fix a tuna-fish casserole for you to pop in the oven. Would that be all right, do you think, Ollie?"

"Sure," I said, not volunteering to help her put it together. Because, after all, since it had been Meredith's idea Mom should go to college, why shouldn't *she* fix the dinners from now on. "With crushed potato chips on top," I added.

Mom came over and put her finger under my chin. "You are happy about my going to college, aren't you, Olivia? I'm only trying to keep up with my brilliant children. Of course, I'm getting such a late start, I'll always be miles and miles behind."

"And what's Pop supposed to do?" I asked. "How's he ever going to catch up?"

11

Mom thought a moment. "It's different for him," she said. "He has a successful business. He's proved himself. Oh, *you* know what I mean."

I turned to look out the window and Mom followed my gaze. "The leaves are falling," she said. "It's really autumn. That's somehow so invigorating." She twisted her head toward the back garden of the house around the corner where the new people had just moved in.

"Ollie, I nearly forgot to tell you. I stopped to meet that new family on my way over to the college this afternoon, just to introduce myself, welcome them to the neighborhood, find out if there was anything they needed. They seem nice and friendly. Their name is Brunelli, and they have a daughter exactly your age. And in fifth grade, too. Maybe you'd like to call for her tomorrow morning. She might be in a different class but at least you could walk to school together. What do you think?"

"Sure," I said grouchily. "Why not? I've got to go to school anyway, don't I?"

Mom, who had started for the door of my room, turned and looked at me oddly. "What's that supposed to mean? Of course you have to go to school. You're not even eleven. Not until December. You've got years and years of school ahead of you. The same as Meredith and Greg. And college, of course."

"That's just great," I said disgustedly. "School,

school, *school*! It's going to be my whole life around here, I suppose. In fact, you could even say it was my JOB!"

"You could," Mom agreed, still puzzled. "Anything wrong with that?"

"Don't you understand?" I replied irritably. "I don't *want* to have to do everything that Meredith and Greg . . ."

I stopped short. Mom wasn't listening at all. She had caught her reflection in the long mirror of my vanity table, which I'd recently inherited from Meredith when she'd redone her room into a studio.

"Yes, a skirt definitely, I think," Mom was saying to herself, as she swiveled slowly from side to side in front of the glass. "The first time anyway. After that, I can probably ease into pants. Maybe even, after a while . . . jeans." She lifted her palm to her cheek and cocked her head at her new schoolgirl image.

2

At quarter past six I took the tuna-and-potato-chip casserole out of the oven, and Meredith and I sat down at the kitchen table to eat.

"What's this glop?" Meredith wanted to know, swishing her long brown hair behind her. Meredith's hair was one of her best features. When it was freshly washed it had a nice sheen and a faint wave, like soft, rippling water.

"It's not glop," I said defensively. "If you don't like it why don't *you* start making dinner on the nights Mom goes to school?"

Meredith ignored that. "I'd much prefer a salad," she said, "of crisp raw vegetables. Or a wedge of good cheese with a loaf of French bread."

"Or a jug of wine. And thou," I teased. Meredith

14

had tacked some verses from Omar Khayyám, in a framed plaque, up on the wall of her room.

"Very funny, I'm sure," she remarked.

I dug into the casserole enthusiastically as if to prove it wasn't glop after all. "Thish shtuff is rib-shticking," I told her, having taken too big and too hot a mouthful. I managed to swallow some of it. "And you have to remember, Merrie, Pop likes rib-sticking food. We have to be sure to leave nearly half of it for him. He'll be home around seven. Poor old Pop."

Meredith, who had just started on her food, put down her fork and tossed her hair back. "Olivia, what's eating you? Don't you approve of Mom's going to college? Are you resenting it?"

"No," I replied, busying myself over my plate. "Why should I? If she wants to spend her time reading dull books and doing stupid homework assignments for some crochety old professor, that's her business."

Meredith pursed her lips. When she did that all her other features seemed to wrinkle up, too, until her face began to look like a prune. "That's a ridiculous statement. It's not in the least what college is like. Or any kind of school these days, for that matter. You're talking about the Dark Ages."

"Oh, really?" I challenged. "Okay then, how about this?" I leaned forward, whipped Miss Kilhenny's English-assignment words out of the back pocket of my jeans, and tossed it across the table to Meredith. "Quick," I said, "let me have a one-page story using all these words. And it had just better make sense, or else. If that isn't a Dark Ages type assignment, what is?"

Meredith picked up the list and ran her eyes quickly over it. She was just opening her mouth to say something when the front doorbell rang.

"Be right back," I said, hopping to my feet.

Who could it be? It was still too early for Pop, and anyhow he had a key and usually came in the side door. I peeked out through one of the living-room windows that gave me a good view of the front stoop. (You couldn't go around opening doors to just anybody these days.)

No sooner had I parted the curtain than I jumped back in surprise. There was a pair of eyes staring up at me, eyes that belonged to somebody who'd been standing under the window and trying to peek inside through the space at the bottom of the curtain. The next instant the eyes were gone and I could see a person of about my height run around to the front stoop and up the steps toward the front door.

"Who is it, anyway?" Meredith called from the kitchen.

"I don't know yet," I called back in a loud whisper. "They rang the bell, then tried to look in the window. Now I think they're back on the stoop. Better come see."

Merrie came and peered out the window to check on exactly who was at the door. "It's a girl around your age. Must be one of your friends."

I started to say, "I don't think so," but Merrie had already begun opening the door and the next moment I heard a breathless and slightly cracked voice saying, "Does a girl named Olivia live here?"

I pushed in front of Meredith. "That's me," I said. "Who are you?"

"Me, I'm Anita." She aimed a forefinger at the center of her chest. "I only just moved in around the corner. This afternoon." She pointed a finger in the direction of the house around the corner. "Your Mom came over today and told my Mom about how you were in fifth grade and all."

"Oh, sure, I remember," I said, opening the door wider. "Come in." Meredith had already slipped back into the kitchen. "You're Anita . . . Anita . . ." I couldn't think of the name Mom had said.

"Brunelli," she answered flatly. "Mind if I sit down a minute?"

"No, of course not." I flicked on another lamp. "That was my sister," I said, looking after Merrie. "She and I were just eating supper."

"We're goin' out to eat in a little while," Anita said, "so I can't stay long. Italian. We eat it all the time at

17

home but we like it anyway. Maybe I'll have scungilli."

I sat down on the sofa next to Anita. "Is that like spaghetti?" I asked.

"No," she said in that same flat tone, her voice hoarse and a little crackly. "It's snails."

I made a face and Anita just grinned and shrugged. She was a little bigger all around than I was and had long black hair that curled into ringlets and reached to her shoulders and down her back. She wasn't pretty exactly, mainly because her nose was longish, with flaring nostrils, but I guess you could say she was attractive. By far the most noticeable part of her was her chest. She was undoubtedly far, *far* ahead of me in that area.

"You've got a pretty nice place here," Anita remarked, looking around the living room. "Wait till you see how ours looks when we get it fixed up. The living room's gonna be Spanish. With high-backed red-velvet chairs and a black wrought-iron gate across the entrance."

"What for?" I asked. "Have you got a dog? Or a cat?"

Anita shook her head. "No. No reason. It's just a decoration. That's the style. My Mom's got it all picked out. You'll see."

I nodded, slightly puzzled. Anita was still looking around the room but she wasn't saying anything

18

now. I glanced toward the kitchen where I could hear the teakettle whistling for Meredith's ginseng tea, which wasn't tea at all but was made from some kind of ground-up root that grew in Korea and smelled like wet earth. I wondered what Anita had really come for and how much longer she was planning to stay.

"Well, it sure was nice of you to come around to say hello," I began. Then I remembered Mom's suggestion. "Maybe you'd like for us to walk to school together tomorrow morning. Is that what you came over about?"

Anita's eyes brightened. "Yeah," she said, "I'd like that. And there's something else maybe you could help me with." She reached up, unbuttoned one of the patch pockets of her blouse, and took out a school registration card. "I'm in fifth grade like you. I guess you know. But, see, they only gave me the room number. They didn't say what class or what teacher." Suddenly she reached over and grasped my wrist. "Oh, I'm so scared. Honestly, Olivia. I hope it isn't a strict teacher. You know, some mean old bird. I always have such a hard time at school."

I looked at her surprised, took the card from her, and stared at the room number. "Room three twenty-four," I read slowly.

"Yeah," Anita breathed. "Do you know which class that is? Do you know what kind of teacher they have? Not a man teacher, I hope. We had one in fifth grade in my old school. But I didn't have him. Was I glad. He kidded around too much. It was embarrassing. See, I hate coming into a class in the middle of the year. All the kids stare. You know how it is. Do you think I'm too self-conscious?"

There were actually little sparks of terror in Anita's eyes. She was holding her hands up near the patch pockets across her chest, with the backs out and the fingers curled inward. If she meant that she was self-conscious because her chest development was so much bigger than that of most kids her age, I certainly couldn't blame her. Suddenly I liked Anita very much. She seemed warm and natural and honest, and in need of a friend.

I handed the card back to her. Her eyes were fixed on me and still had a scared, waiting look. I patted her arm. "Relax, Anita," I said. "You're in my class."

She smiled for the very first time and dimples flickered in her cheeks. "I am?" At once she reached out and hugged me. "Oh, boy, that's great. What a relief! Am I glad I came over to ask you. Now I won't feel like throwing up after I eat my dinner tonight. The teacher's okay, huh?"

I hesitated. "She's okay," I said at last. It wasn't really a lie. Maybe Miss Kilhenny would be easy on Anita. Maybe Anita didn't have too much "potential." But of course I couldn't ask her how much she had. "Miss Kilhenny's oldish," I added, "and not exactly fun and games. She *is* a woman teacher, though. And on the whole I guess she's okay."

Outside an automobile horn beeped twice and Anita jumped up. "You know," she said, as I walked her to the door, "I'm not even too worried about the teacher anymore. Just knowing one kid in the class is going to be a big help."

"Right," I agreed. "I'll ring your bell at quarter past eight tomorrow morning. Be ready, though."

"You bet." Anita skipped down the front steps. There was a car waiting at the curb. It was long and sleek, with the dim lights on and the engine running. I could make out a man at the wheel and a woman beside him in the front seat. Anita got in the back and slammed the door, and the woman at the front window waved to me as the car pulled away. I guessed that was Mrs. Brunelli.

Back in the kitchen, Meredith was drinking her tea and writing something on a piece of notepaper, the kind that Mom used for her shopping lists.

"A poem, a poem," I exclaimed, pressing my raised palms together in playful admiration. "The ginseng has cleared your head, opened the gates to inspiration, and you're writing a new prize-winner."

"Don't be smart," Meredith advised. "Actually I'm doing part of your homework assignment, squirt."

21

"You are?"

"Yes, I am," she said, still not lifting her head. "Just to show you it's not impossible."

"Not for you, maybe," I replied, sitting down opposite her with my chin in my hands.

"Not for any normally intelligent eleven-year-old. By the way, who was your well-endowed friend?"

"That's the new girl from around the corner. It so happens she's in my class, in Miss Kilhenny's class. And what do you mean 'endowed'? I'm getting to hate all big words. *And* the people who use them when they could say what they mean in a simpler way."

"Sorry," Merrie said. "I guess I was being catty. But she does have exceptionally large and well-developed breasts for a not-quite-eleven-year-old female."

"Merrie, really!"

Meredith looked up. "Well, I couldn't have said it any simpler than that, could I?"

"I know. But don't make fun of her." I leaned forward and lowered my voice. "She's very self-conscious about it. She hated the idea of going into a new class where she didn't know anybody because she says the kids always stare."

Meredith finished writing and pushed the sheet of notepaper toward me. "Well, you can't do much to protect her. Anyhow, she looks like she can take care of herself."

I turned the paper around to face me and started to read:

In years to come, we will *reminisce* about the eclipse we witnessed last night. During this *phenomenon,* the moon was partially *obliterated* by the shadow of the earth falling upon it.

I read the sentences over to myself a few times. "Okay. Fine," I said. "But what do I do with *collaborate, eject,* and *potential*?"

"My dear," Merrie said, getting up from the table and going over to the sink with her cup, "you don't expect me to do *all* your homework assignment, do you? I did half. Isn't that enough?"

"I know," I objected. "But you took the three easiest words. You left the hard ones for me."

Merrie turned. "If I'd taken the other three, you'd have said that *those* were the easy ones. Come on, Olivia. Shape up. You can do it."

I flicked the piece of paper away from me. "I'm not so sure," I said. "But even if I could, why should I? It's a stupid assignment. Just something to make me sweat more. And if I do special work for Miss Kilhenny this time, she'll just give me more of it the next time."

"And you just might learn more."

"Learn more what?" I glanced over at the sheet of paper. "Junk like that? Look, Merrie, I don't want to be a poet or a writer, like you, or a lawyer like Greg, or even a . . . a psychologist or whatever Mom thinks she's going to be when she gets educated. I just want to be . . . normal."

Meredith was leaning against the sink with her hands in her pockets. "You mean dumb."

"Okay, dumb."

"It's dumb to be dumb," Merrie said scornfully. "And it's even dumber to want to be dumb when you're not really dumb. But suit yourself. It's your life." She turned to go upstairs to her room.

"Hey, wait a minute," I called after her. "What about doing the dishes? I set the table and served the food."

"If you haven't anything better to do," she called back over her shoulder, "you might as well do the dishes. Dishwashing is a nice dumb job, just right for dumb people."

"You rat!" I yelled at her disappearing back. "You're nothing but a prune-faced, stuck-up *rat*." I had gotten up from the table. Now I plopped back down again, hot-faced. I'd have plenty to say to Mom about this. And to Pop, too, as soon as he came in.

I reached across the table once more for the sentences Meredith had written and for Miss Kilhenny's word list. I crossed off the three words on the list that had already been used and glared at the other three. I could probably manage a sentence about *collaborating* with the enemy, or being *ejected* from your seat in a plane crash, or about Miss Kilhenny's wanting me to use my mental *potential* to the breaking point. But I wasn't going to. And I sure wasn't going to be pushed into combining those words into any one-page story. The sooner Killer Henny found out I was dumb, too dumb to be an example of braininess for the class, too dumb to be one of her pet victims, too dumb to be another Meredith or Gregory Potts, the better things were going to be for me in fifth grade.

I clawed at the sheet of paper with Meredith's writing on it, bunched it into a ball with one hand, and tossed it across the kitchen into the garbage pail with perfect aim.

"You're just going to have to learn," I hissed to Miss Kilhenny in an imaginary conversation in my mind, "that some of us are dumb. Yes, just plain dumb. Dumb like me, Olivia Potts!"

3

When I called for Anita the next morning, the door was opened for me by a sprightly little old woman with tiny, diamond-bright eyes.

"Allo, allo!" she shouted at me, very friendly and with a strong foreign accent. "You come see Anita. She come right away. You come inside!"

I went into the entrance hall which led into the living room which in turn opened into the dining room. The little old lady ran ahead of me and offered me a packing case to sit down on.

The Spanish living room wasn't set up yet. In fact, the room was totally bare, with the walls painted bone-white and the ceiling a dark, autumn-leaf red. Beyond it, in the dining room, there was a large panel of white wall with a half-painted mural on it showing a Spanish-looking courtyard with flowers and potted orange trees and a black wrought-iron

26

gate. There was a strong smell of fresh paint in the house.

"No, thank you," I said, declining the packing case. "But why don't you sit down on it?"

The little old lady shook her head and stood with arms crossed, looking at me and smiling, putting her head to one side and then to the other. She was only a bit taller than I was.

"I'm Gran-mama," she said happily, putting the accent strongly on the last *ma*. She lifted her forefinger and shook it back and forth at me. "No Gran-mama Brunelli. I'm Gran-mama Castellani."

"Oh, I see," I said slowly. I guessed that meant she was Anita's mother's mother, not her father's mother.

Before I could say anything else, Grandma Castellani's head of iron-gray hair, twisted and knotted into a tight bun, spun around toward the dining room. I followed her glance. Standing in front of the mural was a strange-looking little creature with a small, round head, a flattened face, slanty eyes, and a pot belly. Grandma Castellani scowled and in a voice that was suddenly harsh and angry she shouted at the little person who was now smiling, with one finger at its mouth, "What you do! Go a your room."

In an instant the little figure slid away. I was beginning to wonder if I'd really come to the right house (and nervously noting that it was already twenty-five minutes past eight) when Anita came rushing down from upstairs.

She barely greeted me. "Grammah, g'bye," she panted, quickly kissing the little old lady on the cheek.

Grandma Castellani's good spirits had returned immediately. In fact, she came to the front door with us and stood there smiling and waving. "Have a nice time," she called after us. "Say allo a your teach. Hope a she's a nice lady."

Out in the street, Anita wiped her forehead with a handkerchief. She was wearing a short navy-blue skirt (I guess she wanted to make a "good impression" on the first day, like Mom), a white blouse, and a loose sleeveless vest, opened down the front and made of some kind of bulky, colorful embroidered material. It didn't really hide her chest. Nothing could. But it hid some of the details. Anita didn't have any school books yet, of course, only a pocketbook slung over her shoulder.

"Whew," Anita remarked. "Guess why I was late? Guess what I was doing up there?"

"I don't know," I said, saving my breath and walking a little faster because I didn't want her to be late on her first day.

"I was throwing up, that's what. My grandma cooked me scrambled eggs for breakfast, with tomatoes and Italian sausage in it. Could you believe such a thing? I took one mouth of egg and some coffee with milk in it and then I went right upstairs and whoopsed."

"That's too bad," I said sympathetically. "She should have known you'd be nervous the first day in a new school."

"She doesn't know *nothing*," Anita said vehemently, "except 'eat, eat, it's good for you.' Oh, don't get me wrong. She's real good to me. Makes a lot of my clothes, gets up early so she can cook breakfast for the whole family. My Mom usually sleeps late and skips breakfast altogether or just has a cup of coffee."

"Oh," I began hesitantly, "I guess your family is bigger than I thought. I didn't know your grandma lived with you. And then I saw this . . . this other person there this morning. Only for a minute. Then your grandma said something to her and she disappeared. Do you have a sister?"

"Me?" Anita asked, poking a finger at her chest almost as if she were surprised. "No, sir! I'm an only child."

I was more curious than ever about the strange girl or woman I'd seen standing for a moment in front of the half-painted dining-room mural. But I guess I was already being too nosey, and, after all, Anita hadn't so far asked me a single question about my family. Anyhow, we were getting close to the school now.

As we were going into the building through the

schoolyard, we bumped into a few kids from my class and I quickly introduced Anita, to break the ice a little for later on. There was Stevie Gould, who was a math and science whiz, Myrna Crossen, who sat in back of me and was taking up tumbling and acrobatics and could stand on her head with no trouble at all, and Buzz Delaney and a kid named Hughie Rand, whom he usually exchanged spitballs with in class.

Once we were inside the school, I walked Anita to the main office where she was supposed to report before being sent to Miss Kilhenny's room.

"Could you stay here with me awhile?" she urged, after the secretary told her to wait in the main corridor just outside the office door.

"Okay," I said. I still had about seven minutes before I had to be in class.

Anita slumped against the wall, which was painted dark green along the bottom half and coffee-beige up to the ceiling. "I'm *so* nervous," she sighed, wiping her forehead again with the crumpled handkerchief. "Oh," she said suddenly, turning and grabbing my shoulders, "I never even told you what happened last night after the restaurant."

"You threw up, didn't you?"

"No." She was talking in a heavy, cracked whisper. "Something else. It made my stomach do a flip-flop, though. It was scary."

"Scary how?"

"Scary because of the cops. The cops got us."

"Got who?" Anita's life seemed to be getting more and more mysterious and complicated all the time.

"Us. My father and my mother and me. We were in the car, see? Driving home from the restaurant. It was only a short distance, because we went to "Pietro and Luigi's" down on the Boulevard. You know that place, don't you?"

I shook my head no. Maybe I'd passed by it but I'd never eaten there. "Why did they stop you? Were you speeding?"

"No." Anita was clutching her handkerchief and whispering urgently. "Not that. It was because of our license plates."

"There was something wrong with them?"

"Yeah. They were missing. Front and back. Gone."

"Gone?"

"Yeah. Stolen, we think. While we were eating. The cops took the number from my father's auto registration and then they let us go. We have to get new plates now, unless the old ones turn up. Crazy, isn't it? First day in our new house and all."

"Weird," I agreed. "Why would somebody steal the license plates off a car?"

Anita shrugged. "Search me."

Just then the office door opened and the school secretary came out and beckoned Anita in. "And where do *you* belong?" she asked me sharply.

"In Miss Kilhenny's class," I answered. I looked toward Anita. "I was just keeping her company until . . ."

The secretary didn't let me finish. "Well, get yourself there. Now. And *no* dawdling."

I felt my face flush and walked away without saying a word.

By a quarter past ten, Anita still hadn't arrived in the classroom, and I was beginning to wonder if she'd been put in another fifth-grade class after all. Miss Kilhenny had started the morning off with math, reviewing the homework (which I'd done) and going on to a new math lesson. Then she started in on social studies. We were taking up Latin America this year and I got Ecuador for my report. Luckily, we drew for the countries by lots, out of an overturned Mexican sombrero that Miss Kilhenny had brought back from a trip she'd taken about twenty years ago. Otherwise, I'm sure she'd have assigned me Brazil and expected me to tackle it single-handed. As it turned out, Brazil was being shared by a committee of three.

We had just finished the drawing when one of the office secretaries, with a folder under her arm (the same secretary who'd been so snippy to me), opened the classroom door and motioned to Miss Kilhenny to come out into the corridor.

"On your best behavior, class," Miss Kilhenny cautioned, carefully placing the emptied Mexican hat up on top of one of the tall clothes closets.

But of course the instant she had closed the door behind her, the whole class was straining out of their seats, craning their necks toward the hallway, and asking everybody else, "What's up? What's up?"

After this had been going on a while, I said, in a fairly quiet voice, "I think I know." In a flash I was the center of attention, with everybody crowding around my desk.

"Big deal," Hughie Rand said, disgustedly walking away from the huddle after I'd told them all about a new girl being transferred into the class. "I thought maybe Kilhenny was gettin' transferred *out*."

"You must be dreamin'," said Buzz Delaney. "Nothin' like that could ever happen. She's here to stay."

Since I couldn't think of anything else to tell the kids gathered around my desk about Anita herself, I added, "Her family only moved into the neighborhood yesterday and already they had a weird happening."

"Like what?" Stevie Gould challenged.

I told them about the front and back license plates disappearing from Anita's father's car the night before while they were at the restaurant.

"That's pretty crazy," Stevie said, getting interested. "Nobody could use those things because the numbers on them have to match the ones on the car owner's license. So why would somebody steal them?" He waved a hand. "Aw, it's probably just some neighborhood kids' idea of a prank. A pretty moronic one, too, if you ask me."

"Unless," Hughie said, coming back into the circle again, "they got enemies. They got any enemies?"

I shrugged. "How should I know?"

Buzz Delaney pushed his way deeper into the crowd. "Lithen," he said, breathing hard and getting his tongue caught between his teeth (he used to lisp regularly when he was younger), "gettin' your license plates stolen, that's nothin'! Guess what we had stolen from us last summer? Our TV, our color TV. Some guys musta come in the house and walked right out with it while my Mom was at work down at the Super Bee and I was over at the "Y" day camp. My Mom only just got enough money together lately for makin' a down payment on a new one. It's comin' soon."

Mrs. Delaney was a widow and worked at the local supermarket as a full-time cashier.

Myrna Crossen gulped. "You mean to tell me you've been without a color TV all this time? How could you stand it?"

Buzz hung his head. "Aw, there's nothin' good on in the summertime. Anyway, my brother got me a

34

little one, black and white, to make up for it in between. It was okay."

Just then the door opened, everybody scurried back to their desks, and I was actually relieved to see Miss Kilhenny walk into the room with Anita in tow. Anita looked pale, her complexion almost greenish.

"Class," Miss Kilhenny said, tapping sharply on her desk even though the room had fallen into an astonishing silence. "We have a new student. Her name is Anita Brunelli and I want you to welcome her and make her feel at home."

A few kids lifted a hand in greeting and there were a couple of murmurs of "Hi." From somewhere near the back of the room there came a soft whistle. Anita blinked rapidly and looked down at the floor.

Miss Kilhenny ignored the whistle. "I'm sorry all this has taken so long," she went on, "but not all of Anita's records have arrived yet from her previous school, and we've been in the office trying to straighten matters out. I hope you've used the time profitably, familiarizing yourselves with the map of Latin America."

Miss Kilhenny rearranged some papers on her desk and wrote Anita's name in her attendance book. "Now," she said, turning to Anita who was still standing beside her desk, looking down at the floor more embarrassed than ever, "where would you like to sit?"

Anita looked like she was ready to sit anywhere,

including the floor, just so she could stop being the target of about twenty-six pairs of staring eyes. I was hoping she'd choose the empty desk in the front of the room next to short, nearsighted Zelda Barton. That way, most of the class would have only her back to look at. But even before Anita could answer, Miss Kilhenny made the decision for her. Of all places, she sat her in the corner at the back of the room where everybody could easily get a view of the front of her, using the excuse that they were turning around to study the map of Latin America which was hanging on the wall right above her.

While Anita was getting settled at her new desk, and everyone was shifting around in their seats restlessly, Myrna Crossen tapped me sharply on the back to tell me that "such big you-know-whats are absolutely terrible if you want to be a gymnast."

"I don't think she wants to be a gymnast," I replied coldly. "What's so great about standing on your head, anyway?"

"No talking, *please*." Miss Kilhenny ordered. Then she announced that since we'd lost most of the social studies period anyway, we'd just go on to the English homework assignment. "This will give our new student a chance to see the high caliber of the work we do in this class," she said, as she carefully rewrote the five assigned words on the blackboard.

Then, standing there with the chalk in her hand,

she went on talking to the class in general but with her eyes fixed on Anita. "What we aim for in this class," she said pointedly, "is to develop each and every one of you to your fullest potential, to milk your possibilities, to make sure your juices are flowing abundantly."

I could hear suppressed snickers and chuckles starting up all around the room, and somebody even made a soft, mooing noise like a cow. Every eye, following Miss Kilhenny's gaze, was now riveted on Anita's ashen face and terrified eyes. Anita herself seemed to be sinking lower and lower behind her desk, like someone being sucked down into quicksand and actually trying to hurry up the process.

Would Miss Kilhenny ever stop? Didn't she realize how she was embarrassing Anita? Couldn't she hear the mooing that was now clearly coming from Hughie Rand, see the fiery-orange blush on Buzz Delaney's freckled cheeks, the wide-eyed frozen smile on Myrna Crossen's lips?

"Yes," Miss Kilhenny went on, "the key word in this class is *potential*. And now, for the benefit of our new student and all the rest of us, I'd like to call on one of our better English students to read us her very challenging and valuable homework assignment. It should set an example for all of you as to what can and will be accomplished in our fifth-grade class this year."

The snickers and murmurs died down at last and a deep hush fell over the entire classroom.

"Olivia Potts," Miss Kilhenny commanded, "please stand and read us the one-page story you wrote."

4

It was half-past three by the time Anita and I finally left school that afternoon.

Anita had been kept back so that Miss Kilhenny could take her to the bookroom and the supply locker and load her down with textbooks and work-books and all sorts of instructions and advice and reading assignments. She wanted Anita to brush up on some extra work to make up for the month of fifth grade at our school that she had missed.

I, of course, was kept back so that I could explain to Miss Kilhenny why I had not done my English homework assignment and had thereby let her down "so inexcusably." Finally, she'd let me go, after I'd turned coward and done a lot of sheepish mumbling

39

about how I didn't have "enough time last night." Only this time, Miss Kilhenny had given me a double assignment—the six old words and five new words, eleven altogether, to put into sentences—to make up for not doing yesterday's special assignment.

"But I don't really think that's fair," I complained, as she made me sit down to copy the five new words. They were:

procrastinate
exacerbate
relevant
succulent
ambulatory

"Please explain what you mean by that, Olivia."

"I mean, uh . . . Miss Kilhenny, that I'm still being given extra work. And I don't see why. If I was anybody else in the class, I'd have had to put the five old words in sentences and that would be that. This way, it's like . . . like I'm being punished for having been punished."

"So you consider learning to be punishment, do you? That's a very strange attitude coming from someone in a family like yours."

"But I'm not really like Gregory or Meredith. Or . . . or even my mother. I just might take after my father's side of the family." (Pop actually did have a younger brother who was "a little bit retarded.")

"School's really harder for me, Miss Kilhenny, than it was for my sister and brother." I wouldn't have dared tell her about my mother just starting in at college.

Miss Kilhenny smiled her grinning, death-mask smile. "Excuses, excuses. I know the difference between laziness and a dull mind. And believe me, I know your IQ, my dear. I'll save you from bad work habits and bad influences in spite of yourself. You'll see."

What did she mean by "bad influences"? But I could see it was useless to go on complaining, so I copied the words while Anita waited at the back of the room. Then she and I set off for my father's gas station, both of us loaded down with books that Miss Kilhenny had given Anita. Anita was carrying eight and I was carrying another three, plus my own of course.

"Are you *sure* it's shorter to this place than home?" Anita asked as we trudged along, stopping every now and then to put the books down on the hood of a parked car or some other flat surface and shift their weight around. "I *know* we're walking in the opposite direction from where we live and it seems so *far*."

"Believe me, it's shorter," I answered soothingly. "My Pop clocked it. It's seven-tenths of a mile from our house to the school and only four-tenths of a mile from the school to my Pop's station."

"And what if there's nobody at the gas station to drive us home?" Anita worried, hoisting the books higher in her arms.

"There will be, there will be. It's not just a regular gas station. I told you. They do lots of repairs and rebuilding engines and stuff. The place is always loaded with cars."

"Yeah, all busted," Anita remarked, tripping on a piece of broken pavement.

"I promise you we'll ride home the minute we get there," I insisted wearily. "Gee, I know we both had a rotten day, Anita. I almost think mine was worse than yours. I've got the eleven hardest words in the whole English language to put into sentences—'*intelligent* sentences, sentences that will tell us the *meaning* of the word . . .' "

"So what?" Anita interrupted. "I went through plenty, too."

"I know," I said, instantly sorry. "Was it awful the way they were looking at your . . . your . . ." I couldn't even bring myself to say the word *chest* to her.

Anita tossed her head. "I've had worse experiences." Maybe Anita hadn't even heard the sound of mooing, or at least not recognized it. She sighed. "It's like I told you. Kids in a new class or something like that always stare at me. Well, at least the worst is over. My Aunt Bea says I'm too self-conscious. She says I only imagine it. Well, what's the dif?"

I could see she didn't really want to talk about it. She gave the books in her arms another useless hoist. "It's all this stuff she wants me to read that's really got me down now. How can I do it all? I get so restless reading. The words all begin to look like nothing but dirt marks on the paper."

"Who's your Aunt Bea?" I asked nosily, ignoring Anita's other complaints. "Is she the person I saw in your house this morning?"

Anita looked at me with a flicker of alarm in her eyes. But she answered me very smoothly. "No, my Aunt Bea doesn't live with us. She's my *father's* sister. She has a part ownership in a beauty stop. The "Beauty Boo-Teek," it's called. Just off the Express-way, near where it crosses the Boulevard. I'm sure you know that place."

"Uh-uh." I shook my head.

"Well, anyhow, one of the real reasons I don't care about school and that people like Miss Kilhenny can't get me to work hard is that I'm only going until I'm sixteen and then quit. Because I'm going to be a beautician. My Aunt Bea's already teaching me how to comb and cut and set wigs. See, they sell wigs at the Boo-Teek, too. Fantastic. Say, did you ever try on a long red wig with just a slight dip over the eye and a flip all around the bottom? Or a real tight, curly, frosted one? It's sensational. Makes you feel like a different person. Like you could do anything or be anything. A country music star, maybe, or . . . or a rock singer."

It was the first time I'd seen Anita so carried away. "I never tried on any wig at all," I answered. "I never even thought about it."

Anita grabbed my arm. "We'll go there. Day after tomorrow. Saturday. I'll show you the whole place. Introduce you to my aunt. She's terrific—just like a big sister to me. Oh," Anita moaned, "if only I was sixteen already. I could be earning my own money, doing anything I liked. 'No more classes, no more books, no more teachers' dirty looks.' "

Anita kicked a bottle cap along the sidewalk. "Believe me, I don't need to knock myself out studying spelling and grammar or the map of South America to run a beauty shop and sell wigs. All I need to know is how to add and subtract and work the cash register and keep track of stock, and I already know all that. And plenty more. I'm just naturally good with numbers."

I sighed. "Well, for your sake I hope you have a low IQ."

Anita stared at me.

"An IQ," I repeated. "An intelligence quotient, the mark you get when they give you an intelligence test."

"I know what it is," Anita said. "But why? Why do you wish I have a low one?"

"Well, do you?" I asked back.

Anita shrugged. "How should I know? They never tell you."

"I know, it's secret," I agreed. "But sometimes it does leak out by accident. Anyhow, they keep that information in your records and pass it on from one class to another and from one school to another. And if it's high, the teachers work you much harder. That's what Miss Kilhenny's always talking about when she yammers at us about our 'potential'. If your IQ's low, though, then they figure they can't do too much with you and they leave you alone more. All you have to do is just get by with passing grades."

"That's for me," Anita said. "That's all I want." She turned to me. "How about you? What's your IQ? High or low?"

I glanced at her hesitantly for a moment. "How should I know?" I shrugged. "You know as well as I do. It's a secret."

We were approaching my Pop's gas station now. It was just across the intersection on a big busy corner. Even Anita was impressed.

"Wow," she exclaimed. "Your Pop owns this?"

I nodded.

"Is he a part owner or does he own the whole thing?"

"The whole thing," I replied. "For years and years. It's one of the most popular stations around. They have their own body shop. You know, for fixing up cars that have gotten banged up in accidents. And they outfit hot rods and stock cars. Everything."

"Um hmmm," Anita mumbled appreciatively.

As we cut across past the gas pumps, I could see Pop sitting in the big, glass-enclosed office. One door led into the office from the outside and another led directly from the office into the shop. Pop was sitting at the big main desk in his shirtsleeves, his collar open and his tie pulled to one side.

Since the business had become more and more successful and he'd hired a shop foreman and so many mechanics and attendants, Mom had insisted that he wear a clean white shirt to work every day. But of course he still pumped gas if they were short-handed and sometimes, in an emergency, he even got down on one of the low wooden dollies and slid under a car to take a fast look at what was wrong underneath. Then he would come home, show the filthy white shirt to Mom and say, "I told you you'd never make a silk purse out of a sow's ear, Dolores. I should be wearing a workshirt to the station, old sweetheart."

Mom would usually just take the shirt away from him with a smile, put it to soak in stain remover, and quietly answer him, "Well then, how would anybody know you were the boss, Ralph?"

And he'd just grin back at her and reply, "They'd know. They'd *better* know."

It was amazingly neat and clean inside the office, and there was a Coke machine and a water cooler. Pop looked up with a warm, surprised smile when I walked in and I dropped my books and went right over and hugged him. Then I introduced him to Anita and, after we'd parked all our books on one of the wide window ledges, we went over to get ourselves a couple of Cokes from the machine.

Pop started to get to his feet. He was a big man with brawny forearms and thick, shining, reddish-brown hair. "Got to go into the shop for a few minutes," he announced. "You girls make yourselves at home."

"But Pop," I started after him, "we have to get home. We thought you or somebody could drive us. It's late already, and Anita's family is definitely expecting her."

Pop pointed to the phone on his desk. "I won't be long. Both of you ring up right now and say where you are." He indicated Anita. "Better let your girl friend phone first. We don't want her mother worrying herself needlessly."

"He's nice, your father," Anita said, picking up the phone and carefully mouthing her new number as she began dialing.

I could tell it was probably Anita's grandmother who answered the phone because Anita started yelling to her so she'd be sure to understand. Anita's mother, it seemed, had gone shopping for draperies and things.

"A good thing I called," Anita said, hanging up at last with a look of exhaustion. "She was getting worried. You know how she is. 'What you do? Why you no telephono? When you come home? I make a struffoli for you.' "

"Struffoli?" I asked. "Is that something like spaghetti?"

Anita burst out laughing, her dimples flickering. "No. It's kind of like a round, fried ball doughnut that's all sweet and sticky on the outside. They eat them in Naples. That's where she comes from, my grandma. 'Napoli' she always calls it. You don't know *anything* about Italian cooking, do you? Know what, we'll have to invite you over for dinner some time. When we get the house all fixed up, of course."

"Sure," I said. "It sounds like fun. Now I have to call my house. Except I'll be surprised if there's anybody there. My Mom's probably out buying books at the college bookstore or picking up a pair of blue jeans to wear to class."

Anita looked at me in surprise. I hadn't had a chance yet to tell her about my Mom's having just started college. I suppose I hadn't been very sure I wanted to.

The phone at home was still ringing, when Anita

suddenly clutched my arm so hard that her nails dug into my skin.

"Hey!" she shrieked, staring transfixed out the window of Pop's office. "See that car over at the gas pumps? The one that the tall blond guy just got into?"

"Which one, which one?" I gasped, sensing from Anita's throbbing fingers, which were now scratching my arm like cats' claws, that something pretty important was up. "You mean that beat-up old station wagon or that little white foreign car over there?" I couldn't see the person sitting behind the wheel in either car.

"The wagon, the wagon," she pointed, practically jumping up and down. "See the number on the back?"

"Number? What number?" I shrilled, catching her excitement but still having no idea what she was carrying on about.

"The *number*," she repeated emphatically. "Five four seven QJ . . ." The driver had now swung the car forward, then put it in reverse, and was backing up swiftly, coming closer and closer toward the glass-fronted office before making a sharp turn so that he could leave the station by the side street rather than the main avenue.

All of a sudden I could see very clearly what Anita meant by "the number." She was looking at the rear license plate on the station wagon and once more reading aloud the three digits followed by three capital letters. As she read off the third letter she uttered a furious little scream.

"What *is* it, Anita?" I demanded, practically shaking her. "Speak."

She seemed totally paralyzed. It wasn't until the car had vanished completely from sight that she finally answered me. "That license-plate number," she whispered tensely. "It's the same number as ours. It *is* ours. The license plates on that car are the ones that were stolen from my father's car last night."

I grabbed her by the shoulders. "Anita," I said firmly, "how can you be so sure? Calm down and think about it. There are millions of license-plate numbers in this state, in all *sorts* of different combinations. And hundreds and hundreds of them are so similar they look almost exactly the same."

Anita eyed me steadily and shook her head. "I know that, Olivia. But that *was* our number. I'm sure of it."

"How?" I insisted. "How can you be so absolutely sure?"

"I already told you," she answered stubbornly. "And you better believe it. I'm good with numbers."

5

I was far, far too busy that evening to do more than the first five words of the English assignment that Miss Kilhenny had given me. I put the words into sentences that I suppose weren't very good:

An eclipse is an interesting *phenomenon*.
The eclipse will *obliterate* the moon.
We will *reminisce* about the eclipse.

. . . and so forth.

None of the sentences was more than six words long. And most of them came from what I remembered about the one-page story that Meredith had started to help me with.

As for the rest of my homework, I did very little of it and didn't bother to look up a single thing about

Ecuador. Because that was the night the Pottses and the Brunellis really began to get acquainted.

It all happened, of course, because Pop had phoned the police as soon as Anita had "come to" enough so that she and I could race into the repair shop and tell him how we'd seen Anita's father's stolen license plates on an old tan-and-brown station wagon being driven by a tall blond guy of about eighteen or twenty (Anita thought) who had gotten some gas at the station and then taken off in what seemed to be a big hurry. The police took the license number from Pop and said they would send out a police radio alarm to be on the lookout for the car. Then Anita had called her father at work (he owned a building-supply business not too far from our neighborhood), and Pop had talked to Mr. Brunelli on the phone and told him all about what happened. After that, Pop had driven Anita and me home.

"Now you girls just try to calm down and take it easy," Pop advised as we drew up in front of Anita's house. "Once you give the police a definite clue like a license-plate number, they're pretty sure to turn up something."

The moment Pop stopped the car I noticed an oldish maroon convertible parked in Anita's driveway. The first thing I found myself doing was reading the license-plate number. I put my hand over my mouth to muffle a gasp. The number was exactly the same as the one on the missing plates, except instead of five four seven it was five four eight.

This time it was my turn to clutch Anita's arm. Had she been wrong the whole time? Wasn't *this* her father's car, the one I'd seen last night, with the so-called stolen plates right back on it? Suppose the whole thing had been a big embarrassing mistake. Or maybe Anita was one of those people who make up stories all the time just to get attention. After all, how well did I really know her?

Anita followed my shocked glance and my pointed finger. "Oh, that," she remarked casually, after figuring out what was on my mind. "That's my mother's car. She must have just gotten home."

"But the plate number, Anita," I whispered. "It's *almost* like the other one, the one you said was stolen."

Anita wagged her head. "Well, of course it is. Five four eight, that's my mother's number. Five four seven, that's my father's. They always order their plates at the same time, so they're always one number apart. Otherwise, they're exactly alike. What's the matter with you? Don't you trust me?"

I was still sighing with relief when the front door of Anita's house opened and Mrs. Brunelli came walking toward the car. She was a tall, stately woman with broad shoulders and long, dark hair like Anita's except she wore it in a lacquered upsweep with a fancy twist at the back. She probably had it done at the Beauty Boo-Teek. Mrs. Brunelli had large, dark, sad eyes, a long straight nose, and permanent dimples in her cheeks.

"You must be Mr. Potts," she said, reaching into the car and extending her hand to Pop before he had a chance to get out. Her voice was deep and husky. "I'm Rosetta Brunelli," she said. "Or Rose, you can call me. I heard. My husband phoned me a little while ago and told me the whole story. I can't thank you enough."

"Oh, don't thank *me*," Pop grinned. "Thank that little girl of yours back there." He pointed over his shoulder, with his thumb, toward Anita sitting with me in the back seat, our school books scattered all around us. "She's the one spotted your plates on that car that was gassing up at the station. She's got a quick eye, all right."

Mrs. Brunelli peered into the back seat. "Hi, baby," she said to Anita, waggling her fingers at her. Her eyes turned to me. "And you must be Olivia. I'm awfully happy to meet you. I met your Mom the other day. A lovely person."

While Anita and I were still sorting ourselves out, deciding which books were Anita's and which mine, Pop beeped his horn at a car going slowly through the street. The car stopped alongside us. It was Mrs. Delaney, Buzz's mother, who worked at the Super Bee supermarket.

"Hello there, Mr. Potts," Mrs. Delaney called over in her tired, draggy voice, with just the faintest hint of an Irish brogue in it. "Got this terrible throbbing pain in my leg. I told 'em if I didn't get let off early today it was going to be another inflammation for sure. Oh, my, what a life it is."

Pop nodded sympathetically. "Come and meet your new neighbor, Mrs. Brunelli, Mrs. Delaney. That is, if you haven't met already."

Mrs. Delaney pulled her car over to the curb and in a few minutes Pop, Mrs. Brunelli, and Mrs. Delaney were standing in a tight little knot on the sidewalk, gossiping away the way most of the neighbors did in our neighborhood, especially when the weather was nice.

"Now then, isn't it odd," Mrs. Delaney was saying after having heard about the Brunellis' stolen license plates, "how the police never turned up hair nor hide of that color TV set that they stole away from *me* last July? Oh, I dearly loved that TV. And I'd only just made the very last payment on it the week before it was taken."

Mrs. Brunelli's eyes opened wide. "You mean to tell me they broke into your house this past summer and stole a TV? Well, I never. The real estate agent never told us there had been a burglary in the neighborhood."

Mrs. Delaney put a hand to her graying red hair, which was coarse and stiff-looking with jagged, chopped-off ends. She might have been pretty once upon a time but now she had hard, thin lips and deep double lines in both cheeks. "Well, the realty people wouldn't tell you a thing like that now, would they? It kills sales, doesn't it?" Mrs. Delaney turned knowingly to Pop. "But there have been a few little things, now and then, here and there, in the neighborhood, haven't there, Mr. Potts?"

Pop cleared his throat. I think he was trying to get Mrs. Delaney to stop scaring Mrs. Brunelli, and also to notice that I was standing just behind him listening closely to their conversation. Anita had already gone into the house, after being greeted at the front door by her grandmother who had waved to me, nodding and smiling.

Mrs. Delaney seemed to take no notice of Pop's throat noises and went right on talking about the loss of her TV set. "Well, goodness knows it took some doing, and plenty of overtime in the heat of summer, to save up for a new one. And now I've made the down payment and the set was to have been delivered early this week and, wouldn't you know, it hasn't come. I called the store and they said it *was* delivered and somebody had signed for it. But of course that's all a mistake because there isn't anybody home durin' the day except Buzz after he gets home from school. And then he comes right on over to the Super Bee to carry grocery bags to people's cars for a few extra dimes and quarters. And *he* hasn't seen it, so where is it then?"

I opened my mouth to say something, held back for a moment, and then piped up, "What about Norman?"

Mrs. Delaney, Mrs. Brunelli, and Pop all turned to look at me.

"Norman?" Mrs. Delaney squinted. "*My* boy Norman? Well, what about him?"

"Well," I said, swallowing uncomfortably, "I saw *him* around. Just yesterday. While I was doing my homework."

Mrs. Delaney stared at me with eyes like pale-green crystal beads. "Where on earth. . . ? Where'd you see him then?"

"Right in your backyard," I replied. "I'm sure it was he. In fact, I'm altogether positive of it. He was with Harvey Epping. I think. Yes, I'm pretty sure of that, too."

Mrs. Delaney dug her fingers into her hair and scratched her head vigorously. "It's not possible, child. Simply not possible. Norman hasn't been home since early summer. He's working on a construction job down in Maryland. Calls me up from time to time. Such a good boy, Norman. Very steady. He phoned me up, why, just a few days ago. From Maryland, he did. So, you see, you must've been seein' things, my dear."

"I most certainly was not seeing things," I blurted out. What a stupid woman this Mrs. Delaney was anyway. "I know exactly what I . . ."

But Pop had already put one arm tight around my shoulder and pressed a finger to my lips. "Never mind, now," he grinned. "We all make mistakes." He smiled and winked to Mrs. Delaney and Mrs. Brunelli, waving good-bye to them and propelling me toward the car. "Young fellas all look alike these days, don't they?" he went on, half to me, half to them. "Tee shirts, blue jeans, sneakers. Can't tell one from the other. Easy to make a mistake."

Both women nodded. I knew better than to say anything else about it to anybody. Maybe I was dumb, dumber than Meredith, dumber than Gregory, dumber than Mom, dumber even than Pop. But I wasn't so dumb that I didn't know whether or not I'd seen Norman Delaney yesterday afternoon. And I'd seen him all right.

Mom was home for dinner that evening since it wasn't one of her school nights, and Pop and Meredith were home early, too, so we all ate together. Mom and Meredith hogged the conversation and it was all about Mom's two college courses. She'd had her first class in each of them the night before, and she was so excited she couldn't wait until the next Monday, Tuesday, and Wednesday.

"I thought you were supposed to go to school only

two nights a week," I remarked, buttering another hot roll. We were having pot roast with gravy and I realized it was probably a rare last treat.

Mom put down her fork and finished chewing. "No," she explained, pointing two fingers at Pop and me. "You see, 'Family and Community' is a work-shop course. That means a double session for that one. Well, anyhow, it's all just fascinating. I have a lot of reading to do over the weekend, though," Mom passed Meredith a book that she had brought to the table. "The assignment for the social psych course is chapters one through four in there. It'll be heavy going, don't you think?"

Merrie began to examine the book carefully.

"Is that how you're going to spend your weekends from now on?" I asked Mom, stuffing half the buttered roll into my mouth. "Wouldn't you really rather be working on your needlepoint or baking cookies for the next Parents' Association meeting?"

"Right," Pop agreed, playfully pounding the table with his big fist. "Or how about sitting beside me and doing my billing for me on a Sunday afternoon? Eh, love?"

Mom looked from me to Pop and back again. There was a doubtful smile on her face. But before she could answer, Meredith's face shot up from the page.

"That's right, you two," she taunted, "keep on en-couraging Mom to do good works for the benefit of others. How about making up a welcome basket for the new neighbors, collecting door to door for a couple of brand-new charities, being a parent volunteer for the runny-nose set in the kindergarten room? Sure, it's perfectly possible to fill up one's entire life doing things like that."

"Now, now," Mom interrupted, finally finding her tongue and tapping on her plate for attention. "You know perfectly well I've *done* all those things you just mentioned, Merrie. And they weren't so bad. In fact, I enjoyed doing them a great deal, so you can't say they were *just* 'for the benefit of others'."

I lifted my hands and applauded Mom. "Right. That's what I meant. You *liked* what you were doing. So why take on this whole new load of work? Which you might just hate. And which is also liable to make you very nervous."

Meredith leaned forward across the table. "I'll tell you why, Olivia. Because Mom isn't afraid to grow. Because she's open-minded and she doesn't shrink from a meaningful challenge. Because she understands that doing needlepoint isn't a future. It's a pastime. Or maybe you think somebody is so old when they're forty that they don't need a future."

Meredith's words were so stinging and so emphatic that for a few moments nobody said anything. Then Mom broke the silence.

"Oh, I *know* school's going to be rough," she murmured. "But it's true what Merrie just said." She

60

looked around the table at the three of us. "And I really do want my whole family—Gregory included, of course—to be proud of me." Mom's eyes were shining. In fact, her entire face carried a glow. There wasn't anything else I could think of to say.

Pop, who was eating away again, began to laugh. "Three schoolgirls," he chuckled, shaking his head in wonderment. "Here I sit eating dinner with three schoolgirls."

"Uh . . . make that two," I corrected him, with a sour note in my voice. "I'm not really a schoolgirl at heart. I'm just a kid that goes to school. Because I've got no place else to go. And also because I'm forced to."

Meredith gave me a cold stare. "Are you still having trouble with Miss Kilhenny, Olivia? What's with you anyway this year? You realize you're just carrying a chip on your shoulder because you didn't get the teacher you wanted."

Mom looked up in mild alarm. "Trouble? At school? One of *my* children? Impossible. You couldn't be having trouble with Miss Kilhenny, Olivia. Why, she knows our whole family."

"That *is* the trouble," I retorted. "I'm not an individual human being to her, I'm just another Potts. Part of the big brain chain. But don't worry about it. I'm starting to educate her, little by little. Only it's going to take time."

Mom and Merrie exchanged glances and they

both shrugged. I could see they weren't taking my problem too seriously, and Pop had gone off into another fit of laughter over the Potts' "brain chain," insisting that "anybody who could think that up couldn't have too much the matter with their brain."

I dug disgustedly into my dessert, even though it was my favorite—lemon meringue pie—and was just finishing up the last of it when the telephone rang. Pop got up to answer, probably figuring something had come up over at the station. He came back to the table, wiping his mouth and carefully folding his napkin.

"Finish up, Ollie. You and I have to go over to the Brunellis'. The cops are there. They just found the car with Mr. Brunelli's license plates on it."

"Really!" I jumped up, stuffing a last piece of pie-crust into my mouth.

Mom pushed her coffee cup away. "Oh, I'm coming with you, Ralph. If the neighbors are in trouble, I'd better go along and see what it's all about."

A moment later Meredith was the only one left sitting at the table.

"Whatever is all the excitement about?" she asked coolly, slowly eating her pie.

"Nothing that would interest you," I replied, pulling on my jacket. "It's cops and robbers stuff. So unpoetic. But," I added, "there is something you could do while we're gone."

"Oh, really?" Merrie asked suspiciously, beginning to make her prune face at me. "And what might that be?"

"The dishes," I snapped back at her. "As you said to me last night," I added, about to skip out the side door just ahead of Mom and Pop, "it is a dumb job. But sometimes even smart people get stuck with it. Besides, it just so happens it's your turn!"

6

The Beauty Boo-Teek was jammed with customers at eleven o'clock on Saturday morning when Anita and I arrived. Every chair was taken, and behind each chair stood a hairdresser, either washing or setting, spraying or blowing, snipping or clipping hair. Other customers were already sitting in a long row of chairs at the back of the shop, with their heads baking like cakes under the hair driers.

"Saturday's the big day," Anita explained, as we wandered toward the rear in search of her Aunt Bea. "There's parties, weddings, all kinds of affairs. Everybody wants to look good for the weekend. You know how it is."

Anita was chewing gum. It was a warm day for October and we'd taken the bus down to the Boulevard, passing Pietro and Luigi's, the Italian restaurant where Anita had eaten dinner with her parents on the day they had moved into their new house.

"See," Anita had pointed, jabbing a finger past my nose at the smeary glass of the bus window. "That's the place where it all started. And where are we now? No place."

I nodded in sympathy. Night before last, when the police had come to Anita's house to report having found the car with the Brunellis' stolen license plates on it, we'd all thought they were onto something big. But instead all they had to tell us was that they'd picked up the old tan-and-brown station wagon, abandoned down near one of the small-boat docks at the bay. They had suspected that the car had been stolen, as well as the plates, and they'd taken it in for investigation.

"Okay, let me get this straight," Anita's father had said to the cops. This was just after Mom and Pop and I had arrived at the Brunellis' and we'd all gotten introduced to one another. "The station wagon was stolen from *one* party, and the plates that were on it at the time were taken off and hidden away somewhere. Then the plates were stolen from *another* party, namely *me*, and put on the stolen car. All for the purpose of causin' confusion."

Anita's father was a lean, good-looking man with a cleft chin, gleaming black hair, and flashing eyes. He was probably about the same age as her mother, but he looked younger. Some of the girls over at Meredith's high school might even have called him "cute" and tried to flirt with him.

The gray-haired, more heavy-set of the two police officers nodded. "That's it. As far as we can tell right now."

Mr. Brunelli shook his head. "So what were these punks tryin' to do? It wasn't just a game. It wasn't even a joyride. You don't steal a beat-up old station wagon for joyridin'. You steal somethin' fast and flashy. A sports car, maybe one of those fancy foreign jobs." He turned to Pop. "I'm sure my friend here who runs a gas station and has a lot of dealings with these type kids can confirm that. Isn't that right, Potts?"

Pop scratched his temple. "Yes, you've got a point there."

Mom, who was standing next to Pop, linked her arm through his. "But of course we can't be sure what kind of people the culprits were, can we, Mr. Brunelli? They *could* have been adolescent boys, young men, as you seem to think. But we don't really know. Nor do we know why they did it."

"Oh, I can tell you why they did it, Mrs. Potts," Mr. Brunelli shot back. "I own a building-supply outfit and I know all about people who haul off stuff that don't belong to 'em. Happens all the time. They

66

use a station wagon, panel truck, pick-up truck, that sort of rig. I'll bet my bottom dollar those kids were passin' stolen goods in that car, with *my* plates on it. And they *were* kids—well, the one my girl Anita here saw was, anyway." He turned to the police officer. "You get that fella, the one my girl saw, and we'll come down to the station and identify him and press charges anytime you say. You got that?"

The officer nodded. "We got you, Mr. Brunelli. You'll be hearing from us."

But the moment the two policemen had gone out the door, Mr. Brunelli (his first name was Paul) broke into a broad, face-cracking grin. "Yeah, yeah," he mused, his eyes narrowed with amusement, "you'll never hear another word from them. It's a dead end, believe me, just like the dead-end street they found that station wagon on."

A few minutes later, cheery and back-slapping, Anita's father was offering drinks around, making up a couple of Shirley Temples (ginger ale with a cherry and red fruit syrup in it) for Anita and me. "So what?" he said jovially, raising his glass to Mom, Pop, and the rest of us, all standing around in the freshly painted, still-empty "Spanish" living room. "So long as we didn't lose no more than a coupla license plates, we won't complain."

Anita told me the next day that she felt exactly as her father did about it, and she especially hoped they didn't find the tall blond young man she'd seen getting into the station wagon because she would have to be the one to identify him and it would be so embarrassing and maybe even dangerous, too.

I couldn't help agreeing with her that probably the best thing to do was to forget the whole thing and just put it down as a weird happening. The only thing that did keep bothering me, though (which had nothing to do, of course, with the Brunellis' stolen license plates) was that business of Mrs. Delaney telling me I *couldn't* have seen Norman in her backyard a couple of days ago. Now that was really a weird happening.

At the beauty shop on Saturday morning, we finally found Anita's Aunt Bea in a little cubicle hung with pink nylon curtains where she was giving a customer's hair a special "sunstreak frosting." The customer was lying back in the chair with a mask over her eyes and forehead to prevent any of the dye getting on her skin, while Aunt Bea applied dabs of the "streaking" mixture with little pads here and there all over her hair for an artful effect.

Anita's aunt was chewing gum very fast as she talked to the customer, who was telling her all about the cruise to the Caribbean that she was going on, which was why she was having her hair done this way. "So I'll look good even before I get to the islands," the customer was saying.

"Um hmmm," Bea replied, dabbing and smearing, dabbing and smearing. "You're doin' a smart thing. With this hairdo and plenty of suntan makeup, you'll be the classiest-lookin' gal on the ship sailin' down, while all the rest of them still look pale and milky. I only wish all my customers had such good sense."

While all this was going on, Anita had gently lifted the curtain of the cubicle and walked in, beckoning me to follow. I had expected Aunt Bea to be ravishingly beautiful, with all the advantages she had at her command. So I was terribly disappointed to find that she had tight lips, puffy cheeks, a pudgy nose, and a sallow complexion. On top of that, she wore big round eyeglasses and had her hair tightly curled into a sort of squared-off Afro that was dyed a muddy, streaky yellow brown that almost matched her skin.

"Hi, baby," Bea greeted Anita, between chews and only slightly turning her head, while still talking to the customer. "How ya doin'?"

"Who's there?" the masked customer asked suspiciously.

"Nobody," Bea assured her. "It's only my niece and another little girl. Friend of hers, looks like. She's a sweet kid, my niece. Very bright. You musta seen her around here." Bea snickered. "Actually, I'm teachin' her the business."

Anita turned to me and grinned, pleased at her

69

aunt's complimentary remarks. But even after she introduced me to Bea, Bea scarcely looked at us. Everything she was doing to the customer's hair seemed to have to keep rhythm with her gum chewing.

"We'll look around the shop," Anita said, after a while, to her aunt. "I wanted to show Olivia some of the wigs. I won't mess anything up. I promise."

"Okay, baby," Aunt Bea replied, still keeping her beat. "Be good. See ya."

But over at the wig counter, all the chairs and mirrors were taken, and a muscular young man in slim trousers and a tight, printed-silk shirt was combing out a wig that a customer was about to try on. He must have been at the Boo-Teek a long time because he seemed to know Anita quite well. His name was Perry.

"Hello, gorgeous child," he greeted her. Anita blushed and looked at me with a shy grin. "Where's Auntie?" Perry wanted to know, busily combing. "Still streaking Mrs. Saddler?"·

"If that's her name," Anita replied. "The lady who's going on the cruise."

"Ah, right." Perry smiled, showing exceptionally dazzling teeth. "That's our Mrs. Saddler. She's one of our very best customers."

Perry, too, was chewing gum, but in a much more relaxed fashion than Aunt Bea. He danced a short distance away from the seated customer, the wig still in his hand, and said to Anita and me in a confidential tone, "People like that. With money, class. That's the kind of clientele I keep telling Bea we've got to cultivate for this shop. Not those gray-haired biddies who come in four times a year for a wash and a set. Easter, Christmas, one christening, and one wedding. Know the type?"

Anita flashed me a wide-eyed look, an embarrassed smile tugging at the corners of her mouth. She turned to Perry and nodded.

He laughed deeply and heartily, placing one hand on Anita's shoulder and twirling the wig in his other hand. "Of course, you do. You're not your Auntie Bea's favorite and smartest niece for nothing."

He returned to the waiting customer and began skillfully easing the wig onto her head. "Trend setters, people with imagination and flair," Perry was saying now in a loud voice. "That's what this world could use more of." We couldn't figure out if he was talking to us or to the customer.

Anita turned to me a little uneasily. "Hey, you hungry?"

"I am, sort of," I answered. "It's nearly lunchtime anyway, isn't it?"

Anita slipped an arm through mine. "Let's go over to the Hamburger Barn," she suggested. "We can come back here later. Maybe it won't be so busy then

71

and we can try on a couple of wigs."

We just drifted away, not really bothering to say good-bye to Perry.

Over at the Hamburger Barn, a block and a half away from the Boo-Teek, on the Boulevard, it was still a little early for lunch. Anita held a booth big enough for four people, while I went and got the hamburgers, fries, and chocolate shakes for our lunch.

"So what'd you think of it?" Anita asked eagerly, leaning across the table, her fingers bunched around the bulging bun of a double onion cheeseburger.

"The beauty shop, you mean? Oh, fine. Your aunt works hard but she must make a lot of money. It's a busy place."

"The busiest one around," Anita said proudly, diving back into her hamburger bun.

She was just coming up for air when we both heard a short, shrill whistle and looked up to see two familiar figures standing over our table. "Well, well, well, if it isn't old Olive Pits."

"Very funny," I said. It was Stevie Gould, the math and science genius from our fifth-grade class, who'd also been in my fourth-grade class and my third-grade class. He'd been calling me "Olive Pits" on and off for years. Well, what could you expect starting out with a name like Olivia Potts?

The kid with him was also in our class. It was

Hughie Rand, and this struck me odd because Hughie and Stevie were about as far apart in braininess as Norman Delaney and my brother Gregory. They almost never hung around together. They didn't look alike, either, Stevie being short, dark-haired, and stockily built, and Hughie tall and weedy with a pale complexion, a sharp nose, and almost colorless eyes.

Before I could ask them "how come," Hughie flopped down at the table beside Anita, turned to her with a crooked grin, and said, "Yep, just imagine bumping into old Olive Pits, here. *And* Big B."

I could almost feel the hairs at the back of my neck stand up in horror. After all, wasn't it Hughie Rand who'd been mooing like a cow the other day after Anita had been transferred into the class?

"Olive Pits," I said, with deliberate slowness and in a firm tone of voice, "I've heard before. But what's this 'Big B' stuff?"

Hughie smiled mysteriously and turned his head away, his elbow resting on the table and the palm of his hand hiding the side of his face. I looked up at Stevie who was still standing at the end of the table. His cheeks were flushed and his mouth was twitching like he was trying to smother the giggles. Anita didn't say anything at all. Her hands were in her lap now and her eyes were cast down at the unfinished hamburger on her plate.

"You two give me a pain," I said, half playfully, half angrily. With a sudden sweep of my hand, I knocked Hughie's elbow off the table, and the support for his turned-away face collapsed. "Come on, stupid," I added. "Say something. What's 'Big B' supposed to mean?"

Hughie leaped up from the table. He was about half a head taller than Stevie. Suddenly Stevie sat down at my half of the table. He spread his palms out in front of him. "B," he said, muffling a soft splutter of laughter, "B, the letter B. Like in A B C. Simple. B stands for Brunelli. What did you think it would mean?" He looked at Anita for the first time. "That's your second name, isn't it? Brunelli?"

Anita glanced up only for an instant and then quickly looked down again. She didn't answer him.

"So far, so good," I said, picking up my hamburger again and ignoring Hughie who was moving around restlessly. "Now, how about telling us what big's supposed to mean. Hmmm?"

"Big," Stevie said, shrugging ferociously and moving his hands around on the table top nervously. "Big's *big*. What else could it mean? It means, ah . . ." he pointed in the general direction of Anita, "that she . . ."

"Anita," I corrected him.

"That Anita is, ah, a bigger person than you are. Taller, you know, and stuff like that." Stevie looked around the room wildly for a moment. His eye fell on Hughie. "Just the way Hughie, here, is bigger than me."

I peered sharply into Stevie's face. It was surprisingly composed now. His brown eyes looked at me soberly and straightforwardly. But I just didn't trust him. His cheeks were still too feverishly pink. Hughie, too, had made an effort to settle down. He was standing quietly beside the table, his arms folded across his chest and his mouth compressed into a serious line.

"And that's *all* it's supposed to mean?" I questioned Stevie. "Nothing else?"

" 'Course not," Stevie assured me, trying to catch Anita's eye and assure her, too. "Isn't that right, Hugh?"

Hugh nodded crisply. "Right, right. It's just a nickname. Lots of people have nicknames. It don't mean nothin'. Heck, people been callin' *you* Olive Pits for years. Isn't that so?"

I nodded. I had to agree it was so. Even though I'd never been too crazy about the idea, kids—both boys and girls—*had* been calling me that since third grade at least.

"Say, listen," Hugh said, suddenly real friendly, leaning forward with his palms on the table and trying hard to catch Anita's eye for approval. "We fellas actually came in here to eat, believe it or not. So how's about we go and get some food and come back here and eat with you. Would you save these two places for us? Huh?"

I looked at Anita who was now concentrating on sipping at her chocolate shake through a fat plastic straw. "Is it okay, Anita?" I asked. "Would you mind?"

Still sipping, she shook her head to indicate that she wouldn't.

Stevie jumped up and clapped his hands together loudly. "Great!" he exclaimed. "We'll be right back."

We watched them go toward the food counter, bumping playfully against one another with their shoulders and legs, and whispering back and forth with big grins on their faces. All of a sudden, they stopped short and Hughie came bounding back to the table, tossing in a couple of high leaps.

"Just remembered," he panted, slightly out of breath. "Anything we can get you girls? Ice cream? Pie? Doughnuts?"

To my surprise Anita looked straight at him. "Yeah," she answered, her voice crackly and a little hoarser than usual. "I'd like a chocolate brownie with vanilla ice cream and hot fudge sauce on it."

Hughie looked delighted and "wrote" it down across his palm with a flourish, like a waiter taking an order. Anita started to reach for her change purse but he pushed his hand in front of her, palm out, and shook his head to let her know that wouldn't be necessary.

"Nothing else for me," I sighed, wondering how Anita could eat so much. But I guess her grandmother Castellani had her well trained. Except for breakfast on school days, of course.

Hughie vanished and Anita gave me a look indicating that she was feeling more relaxed now, even a little pleased that Hughie was buying her her dessert.

But in my own mind, I was still strangely uneasy. Maybe *I* was the one who was being too self-conscious now, but why did it seem to me that "Big B" referred to one part, and one part only, of Anita— the part that really *was* noticeably big? And why did it also seem to me that "Olive Pits" could, nowadays, very well refer to the part of *me* that was noticeably small?

7

Hugh and Stevie came back to the table with their trays loaded, including, of course, Anita's ice-cream-and-fudge-topped brownie, which Hughie respect-fully set down in front of her. Then they imme-diately dug into their food like they hadn't eaten in three days.

"How come?" I began, watching them carefully and looking back and forth from Stevie, beside me, to Hugh who was sitting next to Anita, "How come you two are spending the afternoon together? I didn't know you were such close pals."

Stevie answered me through a mouth that was full of French fries and oozing around the rim with ket-chup. "Argentina," he mumbled.

"Argentina?"

"Yeah," Hughie offered, tossing back the lank hair that had fallen forward onto his forehead. "You know, the Latin America assignment Kilhenny gave us. Remember we drew lots? Well, Stevie and I got Argentina. It's a big country so she gave it to a team of two people. Brazil has three."

"I know," I remarked glumly. "I have Ecuador. All by myself. Only I still don't see what that has to do with you two. . . ."

Stevie had finally swallowed his mouthful. "Simple," he replied. "We came down here to the Boulevard this morning to see a travel agent."

Anita looked up in surprise. "What for? You gonna *go* there?"

"Nah." Stevie waved a hand at her half impatiently. "Just to get information. Travel folders, stuff like that. They have lots of color pictures in those things. You cut them out and paste them into your report. It really dresses it up. Sometimes you even get a poster. Kilhenny would sure give extra credit for that."

"So how'd you make out?" I asked. I noticed they didn't seem to be carrying anything with them.

"Nothin'," Hughie responded. "We tried this travel place, "Faraway Shores" or something, it's called. They said they didn't have any giveaways."

Stevie shook his head in disgust. "These little outfits out here in the sticks are for the birds. But that's okay. My father's law office is in Manhattan. When he goes to work on Monday I'll tell him to stop by at the Argentina travel headquarters and at some of the airlines offices on Fifth Avenue. I already copied the addresses out of the phone book. He'll get us plenty of stuff."

Hughie turned to Anita. "So what's your country?"

Anita shrugged, her spoon scraping up the last thin streaks of fudge sauce and melted ice cream in her plate. "I didn't get one," she said. "After all, I came into the class late."

"Don't worry," Stevie assured her knowingly. "You will. Kilhenny'll find you some little leftover country in Central America, or maybe even an island in the Caribbean. Or else, she'll put you on a country with somebody else."

Anita moaned. "I don't need it. She gave me so much other work to do to catch up. I have about ten reading assignments. I'll never get through it all."

Stevie dropped Anita and turned to me. "So what's with *you* lately?" He shook a finger at me. "Not doing your homework, are you? Naughty, naughty."

"No, I'm not," I replied stubbornly. "Why should I? Kilhenny's got a nerve picking on me to do extra work. Dumb extra work, too. What's she trying to prove with all that, anyway? That she's some kind of a 'brain maker'? Besides, I've got other things on my mind."

"Oh, yeah?" Hughie wanted to know. "Like what?"

I stared up at the ceiling of the Hamburger Barn, which was all crisscrossed with fake wooden rafters to resemble a real barn. "Oh, like all sorts of weird and mysterious happenings that have been going on around our neighborhood lately." I glanced over at Anita knowingly.

"Like what?" Hughie urged.

"Oh," I said, starting off slowly, "like . . . did I or didn't I see Norman Delaney last Wednesday afternoon messing around in his own backyard?"

"Norman De . . . You mean Buzz's brother Norman?"

"The very same," I answered Hughie, "who, according to Mrs. Delaney, has been working on a construction job in Maryland since the early part of the summer and hasn't been seen around these parts since."

Hughie suddenly pushed his doughnut and carton of milk out of the way, looked around swiftly into the booth behind him, and then leaned across the table to me.

"You're right," he said in a thick whisper. "He has."

"Has what?" I hissed back. "Has been working in Maryland or has been seen around here?"

81

"Here." Hughie drummed with his forefinger on the table. "I mean, up around our neighborhood. I saw him, too."

"Really?" I gasped. "When?"

Hughie thought a moment. "Let's see. I was goin' home from basketball practice. And I was just passing that furniture warehouse about two blocks from the school, next to the vacant lot where they're supposed to build that new playground one of these days . . . ."

"But *when*?" I insisted.

"What do you mean 'when'? On Wednesday, of course. That's the only day I have basketball practice."

I nodded. "Okay, good. Go on. Now *where* did you see him?"

"Gee," Hughie exclaimed irritably. "If only you wouldn't interrupt. Girls gimme a pain in the . . ."

I reached across and punched his wrist. "Never mind. Come on, tell. I have a hunch this is pretty important."

Hughie looked exasperated. "See, you interrupted me again."

"Let him tell it already," Stevie advised.

"What's it all about anyway?" Anita complained. "Why doesn't anybody explain it to me?"

"Aw, shut up, all of you," Hughie barked. But he lowered his voice immediately. "Here I am trying to tell you somethin' that's probably gonna get me into a lot of trouble and you kids won't even let me talk."

We all looked at one another, nobody daring to say a word.

"Okay," Hughie said, calming down. "Now here's how it went. Like I said, I was passing by that place that has the sign on it—FURNITURE WARE-HOUSE, STORAGE, SALES, WHOLESALE AND RETAIL—all that junk, when this car turns in from the street up into one of the driveways that leads into the warehouse. There's this big garage door in the wall of the building, and there's a bell on the side that you have to ring to get them to open it."

Stevie and I nodded. We'd both passed the place at various times, taking the shortcut home from school.

"Well," Hughie went on, "I'm coming along toward this driveway and this guy in the passenger seat starts to open the door of the car to get out. To ring the bell, I guess, so they can drive into the warehouse. I think he musta seen me coming, though, because the next second he closes the door and he sort of slumps down in his seat. But by that time, I'd already seen him and I'd recognized him."

"It was Norman!" I exclaimed softly, trying to suppress my excitement. "Wasn't it?"

"That's right. Norman Delaney. He sees I'm comin' toward him smilin', so now he sits up straight again and he opens the door and gets out of the car fast and closes it. I can't see the guy who's at the wheel because Norm is standin' right in front of the car door."

"And then?"

"Well, then nothin' much. I says 'Hiya, Norm. I didn't know you was back. Buzz didn't tell me.' "

I leaned forward intently, my elbows on the table, my fists jamming into my jaws. "And he says?"

"Well, he says to me, 'Look kid, the reason Buzz didn't tell you is that Buzz doesn't know.' Then he goes on to tell me that he only came back for a day to pay off some debts, he has to see a fella, something like that. And he doesn't want his old lady . . . er, Mrs. Delaney, that is, or Buzz to know."

"Why? What reason did he give?"

"Somethin' about money again. He wants to give them some money but he doesn't have any right now. He's gonna go back down there—where he'd been working, I guess—and save up some more money and come home loaded with presents and all that stuff. I don't know. He gave me this kinda long story. Meantime, the guy at the wheel of the car starts tootlin' the horn real softly. So then he says, 'Remember, don't spoil the surprise, kid. Don't tell Buzz you saw me this time.' "

"And that was it?" I asked

"That's right. That was it. Norm went over to ring

84

the bell in the door and when I turned the corner I looked back and the car was gone. Must have gone inside the warehouse. And that's the only time I saw him."

"On Wednesday." I repeated.

"Yeah, last Wednesday."

"What time Wednesday?" I wanted to know.

"Oh, I don't know. About a quarter past five, I guess. Yeah, I left the gym just a little after five."

Stevie leaned back against the wall of the booth, raised his hands above his head, and yawned. "This is all very interesting," he said, "but it sounds like a bunch of nothing to me. Is this Delaney guy supposed to be a wild kid or what?"

"Not exactly wild," I said. I could clearly recall the scene through the chinks in the thinning tree outside my window—Norman and Harvey Epping pulling the big cardboard carton across the Delaneys' back garden and over toward the front of the garage where I couldn't see them anymore. "More like sneaky than wild," I added. "It seems to me like he *has* to be in some kind of trouble. Otherwise, why wouldn't he tell his Mom and brother he was back up here? I should think they'd be glad to see him even if he didn't bring them any money or presents."

I couldn't help thinking of poor old Buzz who was probably right this minute standing outside the doorway at the Super Bee trying to make a few dollars in

85

small change helping people unload their shopping carts into their cars, while inside Mrs. Delaney was standing on her throbbing legs at the cash register checking out long lines of grocery shoppers.

To my surprise, Anita, who'd been sitting quietly, looking off into the distance most of the time, tapped sharply on Hughie's shoulder to get his attention. He looked up at her from his milk and doughnut. "I don't suppose you happened to see the license number on that car, the one they were driving into the warehouse."

Hughie looked startled. "Gee, no. I never did. I figure the car musta had a out-of-state plate. I'd just guess Norm and this other guy had driven up from Maryland or wherever in it. But maybe not. I don't know."

I immediately realized that Anita was thinking about her father's missing license plates. But that would have been a pretty big coincidence. Still, it started me thinking again. "What about the car?" I asked. "Did you get a pretty good look at it?"

"Oh, that," Hughie said casually. "It looked like any dirty old wagon you'd see around. Just the same as any other . . ."

"Wagon!" Anita and I screeched in unison.

"You mean a station wagon?" I added. "What color? What color was it?"

Hughie scratched his head. "No color," he said

86

flatly. "Color? Why do girls always want to know the color? It was purple and orange with green stripes and blue polka dots. It was . . ."

"Hughie, cut it out," I threatened, "or I'm really gonna land you one."

He laughed. "You?"

"Yes, me," I said. "I've had years of practice on a big brother who just went away to college. So I'm really in training. And all this stuff about '*girls* do this' and '*girls* do that' is a real put-down that's gonna get you in plenty of trouble. With me, for sure. Anyhow, the color happens to be very important. So, put on your little thinking cap and THINK."

Stevie banged his fists on the table and roared. "Hey, Hugh, '*little* thinking cap'. Get that? That's 'cause you have a little head. With a little brain in it. Are you gonna let her get away with that?"

I turned to Stevie. "Oh, pipe down. This is important because it just might have something to do with those license plates I told you about that were stolen off Anita's father's car."

"Oh, yeah," Stevie said, turning serious at once. "What about those? Whatever happened? Did the police track them down?"

Anita and I told about the police finding the abandoned station wagon. Both Hugh and Stevie listened attentively.

When we had finally finished the story, Stevie

shook his head with a grave air. "Well, Anita," he said, addressing her directly for the first time, "I think your father's dead right about suspecting that whoever took that wagon, and then put your plates on it, was doing it to pull a job. You know, to carry stolen goods somewhere."

"But where to?" I asked. "For example?"

Stevie shot a finger in Hugh's direction. "You know where?" he pounced, jumping up in his seat and then sitting down again hard. "To a place like that . . . that warehouse you were just talking about. The guy who runs that place could very well be one of those people that receives stolen goods. After they're delivered, he pays off the crooks, keeps the stuff hidden there for a while, then moves it out and sells it somewhere else, in some other neighborhood. That's what's called a fence."

"A fence?" I asked. It was the first time I'd heard of it. "You mean fence, like in the word *fence*. Like in 'over the fence'?"

"Right. Just like when you toss something over a fence. And then it's gone. Out of sight. Get it?"

I looked at Anita. She seemed as surprised as I was. Hughie was wagging his head, but I could see it was all pretty new to him, too.

"It's the fence that makes stealing the stuff worthwhile for the burglars and other robbers," Stevie explained. "The fence has all the outlets. After all, how's a guy supposed to get rid of a stolen watch or some gold jewelry or a stereo or a color TV? He can't just go stand on a street corner and try to sell it."

I leaned forward, fascinated. "But how come you know all this stuff, Stevie?"

"Simple," he replied. "Remember, my dad's a lawyer. You'd be surprised the things I hear at the dinner table. And a lot of times when he gets private phone calls at home in the evenings."

"Amazing," I said in wonderment, "the way all this stuff goes on right under our noses. Like the world of insects. Or . . . or microbes."

Anita watched me, waiting until I was finished. Then she poked Hughie's elbow with her arm. "So listen," she said, "you never really told us the color of that station wagon you saw going into the warehouse. You just said it was dirty-looking."

"Yeah, it was," Hughie answered. "And streaky."

"Streaky with dirt or streaky-colored?" I asked.

Hughie flung his arms in the air in frustration. "Brownish. Muddy. Dusty. Gee, I don't know. I wish I'd seen it better. I wish I'd noticed the make, the year, the license plates on it. But I didn't. I just can't help ya."

"Okay, forget it," I said. "Anita's the sharp-eyed one and she wasn't there. Too bad."

We began to pile up our trays and load all our

food containers and other junk onto the top tray. The Hamburger Barn was really crowded now and we'd been getting plenty of dirty looks from people hunting for tables and also from the clean-up crew for hanging onto the booth for so long.

Out on the sidewalk, the boys said good-bye kind of abruptly and Anita and I headed back toward the Beauty Boo-Teek.

"You know," I remarked to Anita, "even if that *was* the stolen station wagon that Hughie saw going into the warehouse, your father's plates couldn't have been on it at the time."

Anita stopped and looked at me with a funny expression. "Why not?"

"Because," I said, speaking slowly as though to a not-too-bright child, "your father's plates were stolen at the Italian restaurant that night, probably, oh, sometime between seven and eight o'clock. And when Hughie saw that wagon it was only around five-fifteen."

"That's true," she agreed in a steady voice. "It's also true, Olivia, that we didn't *know* the plates were gone until the cops stopped us on the way back from the restaurant. But they *could* have been stolen earlier that day. Or even the day before."

I looked at her quizzically. "How do you figure that?"

"Look," she said. "The cops don't catch everything

as soon as it happens. It can take a while. And as for the rest of us, who looks to see if their license plates are on every time they get in their car to go some place?"

I couldn't think of an answer to that one. Maybe Anita was having trouble with Miss Kilhenny's reading assignments, but when it came to figuring things out sensibly in her head, nobody could call her dumb.

8

The next morning—which was Sunday—our entire household was thrown into an uproar by a single telephone call. It was a cousin calling long-distance from Florida to let us know that my aunt May Potts, Pop's older sister, had died.

I'd met Aunt May, and Uncle Russell, her brother who lived with her, only once. I guess that was about five years ago, when Meredith and Gregory were closer to my age, and the whole family had driven down to Florida to see Disney World and visit some of Pop's relations. But I couldn't remember any of the Florida relatives too well except for Uncle Russell, Pop's younger brother. He was the one who was supposed to be "slow," "not right," and he *was* somewhat strange and had frightened me a little because he grinned too much, had a high-pitched, unnaturally loud voice, and moved in jerks and spasms rather than in a natural, normal way.

Almost as soon as Pop got off the phone, Mom began tossing things into a suitcase and Pop began calling the airlines to find out about a noon flight to Jacksonville. Meredith was rushing around giving Mom advice about what to take along and digging out a dress for her to wear to the funeral.

"I don't understand," I said, trying to get a word in with Mom and Pop in the midst of all the excitement. "Why do you both have to go? And when will you be back? And won't Mom be missing her classes at college?"

"I will," Mom lamented, looking up from her packing. "And today's going to be a total loss, too. I was going to do all that reading for Social Psych this afternoon. Four long chapters."

"You can still do it. On the plane," Meredith advised crisply.

The phone rang again and Mom waited a moment for Pop to go into the other room to answer it. "How can I?" she whispered back helplessly. "I'd never be able to concentrate. And it wouldn't be fair to your father. Me sitting there and reading while he's thinking about all the problems down there in Florida. . . ."

"Look," Meredith interrupted, "you're going to have to be single-minded about this college thing if you really want to stick with it. And this is a very good example of what can happen. Give in a little here, give in a little there, and pretty soon every little family crisis that comes along will interfere and you'll start falling behind in your work and think about giving it all up."

"Meredith," Mom exclaimed, half-startled and half-angry. "This isn't a 'little family crisis' as you put it. It so happens that May was your father's only sister. She took care of him most of the time when he was little. They weren't close in recent years but they were fond of one another. And now that she's gone, there's this whole new problem. Who's going to take care of Russell?"

"You mean Uncle Russell?" I asked. "Why does anybody have to take care of him? He's grown up, isn't he?"

Mom sighed. "Ah, that's just it. He's probably around forty by now. But mentally," Mom tapped her forehead, "he's only about nine. Younger than you even, Olivia. And he'll always be that way. He can't live by himself. Why, he can hardly hold a job."

Mom gave up on her packing and sat down limply on the edge of the bed. She seemed suddenly overwhelmed.

Meredith picked up one of Mom's blouses, folded

it neatly, and laid it in the suitcase. "I don't see what that's got to do with us." She spoke in a small, tight voice. "They'll just have to make other arrangements for him."

"Merrie dear," Mom said pleadingly, "you just don't seem to understand. *We* are the 'other arrangements'."

Meredith dropped the skirt she'd just picked up to pack for Mom. "You can't be serious. If you bring this . . . this half-wit here to live with us, you'll ruin *all* our lives. Not just your own. How can I have my friends coming here? It's ridiculous." Merrie's face shriveled up into its most prunelike expression, tears spurted from her eyes, and she fled from the room.

I stood there in shock. "Don't," Mom said warningly. "Don't you get started on me."

I opened my mouth to speak. "I wasn't," I protested, when words finally came. "I wasn't going to say anything against it. I was just surprised, that's all. I didn't know anything about it until just this minute. I . . . I don't even remember Uncle Russell very well. What's really the matter with him anyway?"

"He's brain damaged," Mom said, pulling herself together with a determined effort and getting to work on the suitcase again. "Something went wrong with his brain development, probably even before he was born. Nobody really knows. He's not completely helpless, you know. He's good with his hands and he can follow simple instructions. Your father feels he could put him to work at the service station. And he's not dangerous at all. Oh, no, nothing like that."

I went over and put my arm around Mom's shoulders. "Don't worry," I said, brushing my cheek against hers. "It'll be okay. Even Merrie'll get used to the idea. It's about time some of the people in this family realized we can't all be geniuses. And after all, how dumb can he be? I've known lots of nine-year-olds who were pretty smart."

Mom reached both arms around me and hugged me tightly. "Oh, Ollie, I love you for what you just said. I know this isn't easy for you, either. But maybe you can talk to Merrie about it after we're gone. When she's calmer."

I nodded. But I wondered how honest I was really being. Did I just want to show Meredith up for the snob she was, did I just want to make Mom feel better for the time being, or was I really ready to have Uncle Russell become a part of our family for ever and ever?

A few moments later Pop came back into the room. His eyes were reddish and strained-looking. I wondered if he'd been crying. But otherwise he had the same gentle, pleasant expression on his face that he always had, and he clapped his big hands together almost as heartily as he usually did. "All set, old sweetheart," he said to Mom. "We're making a twelve-twenty flight. Harry'll be here in half an hour to take us to the airport. How's the packing coming?"

After Mom and Pop left, the house seemed exceptionally empty. Meredith was upstairs in her room with the door shut. Once or twice, as I went past it, I was tempted to knock. But what could I say to her that wouldn't wind up in a fight? It was hard enough getting along with Merrie lately, even when she started out in a good mood.

Of course, I had plenty of homework to do. I'd been holding back on Miss Kilhenny all week, doing only just enough work to show that I was making some sort of effort, but still not doing the extra assignments. It was part of my campaign to "educate her, little by little." Sooner or later, I figured, she'd either lighten the load or call Mom into school for a "conference," in other words, a showdown.

I knew Anita also had plenty of homework, so I decided to phone her and see if she wanted to come over so we could do part of it together. Anything was better than hanging around in a nearly empty house with mad-dog Merrie locked up in her room and a lot of questions and worries hanging over my head about Uncle Russell and our future family life.

"I can only stay until one o'clock," Anita told me on the phone. "That's when we're having dinner. And you know my grandma. She really cooks up a storm on Sundays."

"I can imagine," I murmured, trying hard to remember what it was that Mom had said we should take out of the freezer for our Sunday dinner. I doubt if Meredith had paid much attention either.

Anita brought over a stack of books and we dumped everything on the bed in my room. I told her about my Aunt May having died down in Florida.

"Oh, I'm sorry to hear it," she said. "So you're all alone here, huh?"

"Yes. Except for my sister Meredith and we're practically not talking to each other anyway." I wouldn't have minded a bit if Anita had right then and there invited me to Sunday dinner at her house. So what if the Spanish living room wasn't furnished yet and the dining room mural was only half-painted? But Anita didn't seem to be thinking along those lines at all.

"What should we do first?" she asked. "Math or English? Math's easier. Maybe you could help me with the English?" She rummaged around and tossed some books onto my desk. Then she sat down on my chair near the window. "Hey, look at that," Anita exclaimed, peering through the glass. "You can see part of my backyard from here. And look, look over there. Right across. You can see all the way into that backyard, even to the screened porch. Who lives there?"

"That's the Delaneys'," I told her. "Buzz's house. And that's where I saw Norman Delaney, his big brother, last Wednesday."

Anita turned toward the window again and leaned forward intently. "You sure have a good view from here."

"Well," I explained, "a lot more leaves fell off the tree in the last few days. But there were pretty big chinks to see through even that day. I could see Norman and Harvey lugging that crate or carton or whatever it was over toward the garage. It was plenty clear."

Anita's eyes opened wider. "What carton? And who's Harvey? You never said anything about anybody else. You only said you saw *him*, Norman."

"Oh, Harvey's this friend of Norman's. They always hung around together. Even in high school."

Anita kept her gaze fixed on the Delaney backyard. "So what were the two of them carrying?"

"They weren't *carrying* it," I corrected her. "It was, like I said, some kind of a cardboard carton, big and square and bulky. Probably heavy, too. They seemed to have brought it down from the back porch. And they were sort of 'walking' it. You know, shoving it along the grass by zigzagging it."

"Well, what do you think was inside the box?" Anita wanted to know.

I shrugged. I hadn't given it much thought.

"A TV maybe?" Anita suggested. "Something like that?"

I nodded. "It could have been. They were being pretty careful with it. It could have been one of those big new color TVs. . . . Hey!" I suddenly shrieked, clapping my hand to my mouth. "I never thought of *that*."

Anita jumped. "Thought of what? What's wrong? Why'd you just scream like that, Olivia?"

"A TV," I gasped. "Don't you see? Mrs. Delaney was complaining last week that her new color TV hadn't been delivered, even though the store said that it had and that somebody had signed for it."

"When was that?" Anita demanded. "What day was it, Olivia? Think hard."

I closed my eyes and clenched my fists together. "It was . . . it was . . . on Thursday. Thursday! The day *after* I saw Norman and Harvey pushing that carton over toward the garage—the day *after* Hughie saw Norman and that other guy driving into the furniture warehouse. Suppose . . . suppose those two had a stolen car parked in the Delaney garage. I could only see a little part of it sticking out, just the bumper, and I wasn't actually watching when the car pulled out of the driveway. Suppose it was a . . . a station wagon, and suppose it even had stolen plates on it. . . ."

"And," Anita said, leaning forward breathlessly.

"And they drove the car over to that furniture warehouse, where Hughie saw them . . . and they sold Mrs. Delaney's brand new color TV to . . . to the fence. Then maybe they hung on to the car for another day, using it for this and that, or whatever, and finally decided to get rid of it, dumping it where the cops found it Thursday night. Now wouldn't that be a very good reason why Norman wouldn't want his mother or kid brother to find out he was back in the neighborhood?"

Anita tapped the eraser end of her pencil against the desk and stared at me. "Do you know what you're saying, Olivia? You're saying that Norman Delaney stole his own mother's newly delivered television set."

I stared back at her numbly. "That's right, I guess. That's what I'm saying. I know it sounds dumb and yet it isn't. After you get over the idea of stealing from your own mother, it's really very smart. She'd be the last person in the world to suspect you."

Anita didn't seem shocked. "And wouldn't it be something," she mused, "if it really did turn out they'd pulled that whole job in that stolen station wagon, with my father's plates on it? After all, they could have. Stolen his plates, I mean. His car was parked in the driveway of the new house all that day on Wednesday, when we were moving in. We were using my mother's car for bringing over the smaller things and the breakables. Because it's older. And there was nobody around at the new house most of the morning while the moving men were loading the truck over at the old house." She sighed. "Still, we'll probably never be able to prove anything."

"I guess not," I agreed. "Only I wonder if Mrs. Delaney is ever going to get her new TV set. I'll have to ask Buzz about that tomorrow at school."

Anita looked at her watch. "Talking about school," she said, "we're *never* going to get any homework done this afternoon. It's a quarter to one already. I have to start getting back."

I pushed all the books to one side and flopped down on the bed. "Hmmm. Me neither. I just can't concentrate. I've got so much on my mind." I sat up with a start. "I might as well tell you, Anita. When my parents get back from this funeral in Florida, I think we're going to have a new member added to our family."

Anita's face took on a really tender expression for a moment. "That's nice," she said, in a hoarse, soft voice. "But wait a minute. Isn't your mother a little old to have another baby? It could be dangerous for her at her age, you know."

"Baby!" I squealed. "Who's talking about having a baby?"

"You are," Anita said blandly. "At least, I *thought* that was what you were talking about. Weren't you?"

"No," I said, almost angrily. "Of course not. What an idea! I said a 'new member'. I meant a new person coming to live with us. A grown-up person."

"Okay," Anita said, getting up from her chair and beginning to gather her books together. "Don't get sore. So I made a mistake. Who's moving in with you? One of your grandmas?"

I shook my head. "Uh-uh, I haven't got any. They're both dead." And I told her about Uncle Russell. As much as I knew anyway.

Anita sat down again. "It's funny," she said, after a pause, "that you should have a . . . a sick uncle who has to come live with you. Because, I guess you know, I have this aunt who lives with us. My Aunt Helen. You might have seen her. She's very short and babyish-looking and she has these little slanty eyes and this little flat nose. . . ."

"Yes," I said hastily, trying to spare Anita having to describe her strange little aunt in detail. "I saw her. That first day when I called for you. Why was your grandmother so mean to her, though? She made her run away."

Anita shook her head. "She wasn't being mean to her. See, my grandma has to scold her a lot because she's so stubborn. And she's nosey, too. She won't stay in her room when she's supposed to. That's why we . . . usually . . . don't invite people to our house. Except for our relatives, of course."

"Why not?" I asked. "Are you ashamed of her? You shouldn't be. And it must make her feel awful, always being hidden away from people."

"Yeah, I guess so," Anita admitted. "But you've got to remember that she's only about six or seven years old in her mind. She can be real mischievous. And then she looks so funny, too. She's what they call a Mongoloid. Could you tell?"

I nodded. "I figured it was something like that. Is she really your aunt? How old is she anyway?"

"She's my mother's younger sister. That's why my Grandma Castellani takes care of her. I'm not sure about her age. But she's over thirty anyway."

"Well," I said, stretching my arms up high above my head and taking a deep breath, "I can see we could be in for a lot of trouble with my Uncle Russell coming here to live with us."

"Oh, it might not be so bad," Anita said consolingly, "if your uncle's more like nine or ten mentally, and if he can go to work, and if he doesn't look too freaky."

"Nine or ten," I mused. "Say, that would be just about the same mental age as Hughie Rand. Sometimes I think he's a *real* idiot. And yet he's in our class!"

We both burst out laughing and I noticed Anita's cheeks reddening into a dark blush. "Listen," I asked her, "what did you think of him anyway, buying you that ice cream fudge brownie over at the Barn yesterday? Do you think it means he likes you or something? Do you like him?"

Anita hunched one shoulder and gave me a silent half-smile. I got the feeling she really did like Hughie a little but didn't want to come out and say it. Funny how she could clam up when she didn't want to talk about something.

"Well, whatever," I went on, "I'd be kind of careful if I were you, Anita. About letting him get away with calling you 'Big B' like he did the other day. I'd put a stop to that right at the start, if you know what I mean."

Anita carefully began piling one school book on top of the other and didn't say anything.

"I . . . I don't mean to get you upset, Anita," I stammered, "but you know what *I* think it means?"

"I know, I know," Anita suddenly exclaimed. "You don't have to tell me, Olivia." And with that she grabbed a piece of scrap paper, slapped it down on the desk in front of her, and with her pencil drew a great big, really huge, letter B. Except, instead of drawing the letter standing up on its base, she drew it in a fallen-over position, with the straight line running across the top.

"Oh, my goodness," I gasped, as she swung the paper around to show me. Lying on its side like that, with the two loops dangling at the bottom, the B

105

looked exactly like a pair of pretty large breasts. It was my turn to blush. I felt so bad for Anita. I could see she'd understood all along what Hugh and Stevie probably had in their minds when they called her that nickname. And yet she'd stood for it silently, made the best of it, even letting Hughie buy her that dessert.

Anita crumpled up the paper and tossed it in the wastebasket. "What's the difference?" she mumbled expressionlessly. "I told you. Don't worry about it. It happens to me a lot."

How thoughtless people were to be causing Anita embarrassment over something like that. They'd probably have been a lot more considerate if she'd had an extra big nose or extra big feet.

But I didn't say anything else to her about it. We got the rest of her books together and I helped her carry them downstairs.

9

First thing on Monday, I passed a note to Buzz Delaney in class: "Buzz, did your new TV arrive yet?"

The answer came back: "No."

I felt like writing "Please explain" and sending the note back to Buzz, but I didn't want to make him feel any worse than he probably already did. Instead I readdressed the note to Anita, writing underneath Buzz's *no*: "So . . . what do you think of *that*?" Then I reached behind me and handed the note to Myrna Crossen to pass on to Anita, way in the back of the room.

We were in the middle of a punctuation lesson. Miss Kilhenny had written six lines of a story from our English reader on the blackboard, leaving out all the capital letters, periods, commas, apostrophes, quotation marks, everything.

"Olivia," she commanded. "Let's see what you can do with line one. Please come up here and put in all the necessary corrections."

I went up to the blackboard and began working with the first line. It was a real mess and, up close, it was harder to decide where the different marks had to go. From the side of the room, someone kept hissing at me, getting me all distracted, and another voice from near the front kept whispering, "Not there. *There*. The apostrophe goes there!"

"Hush," Miss Kilhenny ordered. "No prompting. Regard this as a test. Let Olivia do her own work."

I erased one of the apostrophes and put it somewhere else and changed two of the commas. I'd never felt so nervous standing up in front of the class before. I stood back to examine my work. Finally, red-faced, I put down the chalk and started back to my seat.

"Just a minute, Olivia. Are you *sure* you haven't left something out?"

I stopped halfway to my desk and stared at the string of words again. The quotation marks, the hardest part, seemed to be perfect.

"I'm sure," I said, not really sure of anything anymore. And I sat down.

Miss Kilhenny's lips drew back, exposing both

rows of her small, remarkably even teeth. "Class," she asked, with a real note of triumph in her voice, "what important corrections did Olivia fail to make?"

Several hands went up, a couple of them, like Stevie Gould's, straining at the armpit. But she ignored them, calling on some of the dumber kids first. Naturally, none of them could see anything wrong with what I'd done. "All right," she said, finally calling on Zelda Barton, one of the smartest kids in the whole fifth grade.

Zelda stood up to give her answer. "She didn't put a capital at the beginning of the quotation, Miss Kilhenny," Zelda recited in her prissy little voice. Zelda was a small, dark-haired girl with hairy arms. She was famous throughout the school for her exceptionally high reading score.

"That's correct, Zelda. That and one other thing. Can you spot it?"

Zelda reexamined the words as though she were looking at them under a microscope. Finally, drooping a little with disappointment, she shook her head and sat down.

"I admit the error may be rather technical. Still, an observant student would have noticed." Miss Kilhenny turned to the blackboard and reversed the positions of a period and a quotation mark that I had put in. "The closing quotation mark goes *after* the period." She looked around the room victoriously. Was she waiting for applause, for the whole classroom to stand up and cheer? She was the pettiest teacher I had ever known. I got the feeling she wasn't only trying to teach us, she was showing off to us, trying to impress us with how much smarter she was than we were. And especially how much smarter she was than *me*.

That was on Monday.

On Tuesday, Miss Kilhenny gave us a surprise spelling test of ten new words that had appeared in the previous Friday's English reading assignment (which I hadn't done).

For marking, we exchanged papers by shuffling them like a deck of cards and then giving them out again face down. (Of course, if you ever got a paper to mark that turned out to be your own, you had to report it immediately.) Then, after Miss Kilhenny wrote the ten correctly spelled words on the blackboard, we marked each other's tests.

"Who has a paper that is one hundred percent correct?" Miss Kilhenny asked.

Three hands went up. The perfect papers were double-checked. One of them belonged to Zelda Barton, of course. Myrna Crossen had marked it.

"All right. There should have been many more perfect papers, though. Papers with one word wrong?"

Seven or eight hands were raised. "Two wrong?" "Three wrong?" "Four wrong?" Each time there was a show of hands and, after checking, the owners of the test papers were identified, Stevie had gotten one wrong, Hughie three wrong, and Anita four wrong.

"Any paper with *more than four* misspelled words?" Three or four hands went up. Miss Kilhenny made a disapproving, clacking noise with her tongue. She called on Zelda, who was eagerly holding up the paper she had marked.

"Five words are spelled wrong on this test paper, Miss Kilhenny," Zelda reported, not trying very hard to hide the satisfaction in her voice.

"Really! I'm appalled that anybody in this class should have gotten a fifty on this test," Miss Kilhenny scolded. "Please read out the misspelled words one at a time, Zelda, so that we can check them and make sure."

"Number one," Zelda began. "Resistance. Here's how it's spelled, Miss Kilhenny: r-e-s-i-s-t-e-n-c-e."

"Wrong, of course," Miss Kilhenny pounced, making a single chalk slash-mark on the blackboard. "Continue, Zelda."

Zelda read off four more words, relishing each one, and all with spelling mistakes.

"Quite disgraceful," Miss Kilhenny pronounced. "Zelda, I'm afraid I'll have to ask you to tell us the name of the pupil who handed in that test paper."

"This test paper," Zelda replied, in one of her typical full-sentence answers, "was handed in by Olivia Potts."

Miss Kilhenny's partially opened mouth snapped together like a trap. Her glance barely rested on me. A hand was being waved at her across the room, somebody else eager to squeal on another big loser in the spelling-test sweepstakes. It turned out there were two other dummies as bad off as I was and one person who'd gotten only a forty on the test. Then the papers were collected and we went on to a different lesson.

But of course I wasn't going to escape without some special punishment. The moment the lunch-recess bell rang, Miss Kilhenny asked me to see her at her desk before I left the room. Anita, who was already at my side, shrank away and went over to wait for me beside the door.

"Please have your friend wait outside in the corridor for you," Miss Kilhenny directed. Anita heard her, opened the door, and vanished from sight.

"You didn't read Friday's assignment, did you?" Miss Kilhenny questioned me when we were alone.

I shook my head. "I'm afraid I couldn't get to it. See, there was a lot of excitement in my family over the weekend. This aunt of mine died and my parents had to go . . ."

"When?" Miss Kilhenny asked sharply.

I didn't quite understand her question. "When what?"

"When did this aunt of yours die, Olivia?"

"On Sunday. You see, there was this long-distance telephone call. Sunday morning. That's when we heard of it," I explained anxiously.

"So you had Friday evening and all of Saturday to do your assignment, didn't you? And surely a *little* time on Sunday?"

I peered down at a deep, dirt-filled crevice in the scarred wooden surface of Miss Kilhenny's desk and said nothing.

"This was not one of those extra assignments that you've been complaining about so much, Olivia," Miss Kilhenny reminded me in a vinegary tone. "It was a regular class assignment. You did not do it and now I must give you some special make-up work. If you fail to do it this time, you won't be letting *me* down, Olivia. You'll be letting yourself down. With serious consequences, I warn you."

Miss Kilhenny went to the blackboard, took up a piece of chalk, and wrote out a string of words. She turned around to me. "Now I want you to write a composition on this subject, Olivia. I won't say how long it has to be, but it has to be an honest job with some real effort poured into it. Copy the title. Do this assignment as soon as you get home this after-

113

noon and let me have it first thing tomorrow morning." She brushed the chalk dust from her fingers, reached into her desk drawer for her handbag, and left the room.

I took out my homework-assignment notebook and wrote down the title of the composition I was to write: "Why I Am Not Living Up to My Full Potential in Fifth Grade," by Olivia Potts.

That was on Tuesday.

On Wednesday morning, Anita and I got to class earlier than usual and before I went to my seat I placed my homework composition on Miss Kilhenny's desk. It was in a large brown envelope marked with her name and PERSONAL, because I didn't want anybody in the class to see the title. I'd secretly taken the envelope from Meredith's room. It was the kind she used for mailing her poems and short stories out to magazines. Since she hadn't sold anything so far, even though she'd won that poetry contest last spring and was now editor of the high school literary review, I figured that one more wasted envelope wouldn't matter.

I watched Miss Kilhenny come into the classroom, sit down at her desk, look at the envelope with curiosity, pick it up, open it, and pull out the four stapled-together pages of lined white notebook paper. She glanced up, caught my eye, and put the pages back in the envelope with an air of we-shall-see.

At roll call it turned out that Buzz Delaney was absent. A few minutes later a note reached my desk by way of the "underhand railroad," that is, it was passed from seat to seat by whispering the name of the person it was to go to. Nobody ever looked down as it changed hands. The note was from Hughie Rand: "Do you happen to know how come Buzz is absent today?"

I glanced over toward Hughie and shrugged a how-should-I-know. I had troubles enough of my own this week. Did he think I was Buzz's keeper just because our houses were back to back? In fact, I hadn't even talked to Buzz since Monday afternoon. Anita and I had walked home from school with him, and I was truly sorry I'd sent him that note in class that morning asking whether his TV had arrived.

"Geez, why is everybody askin' me so many questions lately?" he'd complained.

"Who's asking you what?" I wanted to know. But the moment I'd said that I was even sorrier because it was another question.

"Everybody," Buzz had whined in exasperation. "Hughie, for example. Hughie keeps askin' me, 'Hey, you seen your brother Norman lately? What's he doin' these days, anyway? Is he outa town or what?' "

"Well, Hughie's probably just curious," I said, trying to sound soothing and casual. "Um, maybe he saw somebody that looked like your brother or something like that. So he just wondered if maybe your brother Norman had been home for a visit lately."

"Yeah, maybe," Buzz half agreed, jumping out into the gutter to kick at an empty soda can. "Well, what I'd a lot rather see than my brother right now is that new color TV my Ma ordered."

"It didn't come, huh?" Anita and I exchanged glances.

Buzz kept his eyes on the sidewalk. "According to this guy who's the manager down at the Best Bet Appliance Mart, it came all right. Only *we* didn't get it. They musta delivered it at the wrong house and somebody signed my Ma's name for it and took it. Stole it, is what they really did. They had no right. Oh, my Ma's not gonna let them get away with that."

The three of us had stopped walking and were now standing in a tight little knot on the corner a block away from Buzz's street. "Listen now," I told Buzz, "your Ma has to get them to show her that signature. Know what I mean?"

"That's right, she does," Anita chimed in.

"It's the store's fault," I went on. "If they were careless, they'll just have to send out another set. They can't expect your Ma to make the rest of the payments on something she never got."

Buzz swallowed hard. "Yeah, that's what my Ma

says. She says they gotta show her the paper where somebody signed her name. It won't look the same as her writing, will it, so then we'll finally get our set. In a coupla days maybe."

Now, on Wednesday morning in school, it occurred to me that maybe Buzz's TV was coming today and that was why he was staying home from school. I immediately scribbled off a note to Anita to see if she agreed that might be the reason.

Maybe Myrna Crossen did it on purpose and maybe she didn't. Anyhow, when I handed her the note, she scratched my hand with one of her sharp little fingernails. I drew my hand away in a hurry and the note slid to the floor under Myrna's desk, so that she had to go scuffling under her seat to get it.

Miss Kilhenny noticed and said, "Myrna, what's wrong. Sit up straight and pay attention."

Anita finally got the note and read it, and in the flick of a second that I turned to look at her, she made a little circle with her thumb and forefinger and winked to let me know that she agreed.

It so happened that Myrna looked over her shoulder at the very same moment and saw Anita's gesture. Maybe she thought the note was about her. Maybe, even though Myrna and I had never been close friends, Myrna was feeling jealous of my new friendship with Anita. Anyhow, as soon as Miss Kilhenny went to the supply closet for something,

Myrna punched me hard on the shoulder blade and hissed into my ear, "That's the last note I pass for *you*, Miss Olive Pits. I'm not your servant, you know."

I turned around angrily. "Don't do me any more favors if that's how you feel about it, and my name's Olivia Potts, if you don't mind."

Sure enough, Miss Kilhenny heard me. "What *is* the disturbance back there, Olivia and Myrna? Do I have to separate you two?"

"That would be fine with me," Myrna mumbled under her breath.

"If you have something to say, Myrna, speak up," Miss Kilhenny remarked. "If not, let's settle down so we can get on with the lesson. Your work could stand improvement, Myrna. I'd like your full attention at all times."

To my surprise, Myrna stood up at her desk. I could see her hand trembling at her side as she spoke. "I can't *give* my full attention in this class, Miss Kilhenny, when I'm being forced to pass the mail back and forth all day long by . . . by these . . . these people all around me."

Miss Kilhenny looked nonplussed. "Mail? What mail? What *are* you talking about, Myrna?"

"Notes, Miss Kilhenny," Myrna responded in a high, wailing voice. "Notes being passed from this person to that person. Back and forth." Her arms were waving around wildly. "On and on it goes. It never stops. I'm sick of it. Sick of being used, sick of being made fun of, sick of . . ."

"Stop it this instant, Myrna," Miss Kilhenny ordered. It was pretty clear that Myrna was purposely working herself up into a case of hysterics. "I absolutely forbid the passing of notes in this classroom and you all know it. Now, what's in these notes, Myrna, that has got you so extraordinarily upset?"

Myrna let out a really tearing wail. "How should *I* know, Miss Kilhenny!" She extended her arm and pointed a rigid accusing finger at me. "Ask *her*. She's the one who's always writing all the notes and getting all the notes. She's the one who's at the bottom of it all."

There was deathly quiet in the classroom.

"I know that," Miss Kilhenny said firmly, after a brief pause. "You don't think I'm blind, do you, Myrna? Now sit down and calm yourself."

She turned to me. "Olivia, bring all your things and come sit up here, next to Zelda, where I can keep an eye on you. Not doing your assignments is one thing. But passing notes, disrupting the class, and interfering with other people's work is even more serious. After I read your composition on why you are not living up to your full potential in fifth grade, I am afraid I am still going to ask your mother to come in for a conference. Because now we seem to have run into some behavior problems."

Miss Kilhenny gave me a withering look. "What a disgrace, I *must* say, for somebody coming from a family like yours!"

That was on Wednesday.

10

Meredith knocked politely on the door of my room.

"Olivia, come out of there. Or let me in. Or . . . or something." Her voice sounded quavery and even a little worried. I hadn't heard her like that since before she'd won the poetry contest.

"I fixed that macaroni and cheese for supper, the kind you like," Merrie went on. "It's nearly ready. Nice and hot and . . . and gloppy. Oh come on, Ollie. You can't stay in there forever. What will Mom and Dad say? They could be here in an hour. Maybe less if their plane's on time."

I sat by the window chewing on a bloody cuticle and staring morosely into Buzz Delaney's backyard where nothing, absolutely nothing, was happening. I still didn't know why Buzz had stayed home from school that day or whether his TV set had arrived. And what's more, I didn't care.

Killer Henny had gotten to me all right. Or maybe, I'd gotten to her. Because in addition to having changed my seat that morning, Miss K. had read my composition on why I wasn't living up to my potential, during the lunch hour. And she didn't seem to like it one bit. In fact, before I'd left school that afternoon, she'd given me strict orders to have my mother come in to see her the very next day.

I couldn't help thinking how lucky Anita was, knowing that she would be able to quit school as soon as she turned sixteen and go to work for her Aunt Bea at the Beauty Boo-Teek. Meanwhile she could just drift along at school, not working too hard and not being pushed hard either, by Miss Kilhenny or any other teacher. After all, Anita *had* gotten four words wrong out of ten on Tuesday's spelling test and Miss Kilhenny hadn't said anything to her.

Maybe I could ask Anita about getting me a job, too, at the Boo-Teek. Only what could I do there? I didn't know the first thing about setting hair or combing wigs, and when Anita and I had gone back there on Saturday afternoon after our lunch at the Hamburger Barn I'd begun to feel sort of uncomfortable. Aunt Bea was having a quick lunch of a Coke and a sandwich in the same little cubicle where she had been streaking Mrs. Saddler, and Perry was

122

out front combing out a customer's set into a mountain of shiny copper ringlets.

As soon as Anita and I had started for the wig counter, Perry had followed us, shaking his head. "Not today, my dears, if you don't mind," he'd said in a firm undertone, as he gently pushed away the wig on a stand that Anita had been reaching for so I could try it on. "I've got a couple of important ladies coming in a few minutes, and it wouldn't make a good impression for them to find you and your friend here 'playing house'. Do you understand, Anita my darling?"

So I guess I'd gotten Anita into an embarrassing situation, and I could hardly expect to ever get a job along with her at the Beauty Boo-Teek. Oh, well, there was still the chance of being a checker or a stock clerk at the Super Bee, and there was always the possibility of pumping gas over at Pop's service station. Ha! I could just see Mom and Pop's and Greg's and Merrie's reaction to *that*.

Merrie must have realized things were pretty bad when she came home from school around four-thirty and found my door not only closed but locked. So what? She'd been going around with a long face and not talking to me most of the week since Mom and Pop had left for Florida. Now it was my turn.

But my stomach *was* beginning to growl with hunger. So, finally, I dragged myself to my feet, clumped across the room, turned the lock, and slowly opened the door. Meredith's face, pale and pinched-looking, poked itself around the frame.

"Well, well. At last. Such drama. What's it all about, or aren't you going to tell me?"

"Why should I?" I retorted, brushing past her and starting down the stairs for the kitchen. "You never talk to me. And, by the way, what are *you* so cheerful about all of a sudden?"

"Cheerful?" Meredith asked, following me into the kitchen and getting a bowl of salad from the refrigerator. "I would hardly call me cheerful. I'm simply feeling . . . well, normal. But I'm very concerned about you, Ollie." Unlike Mom, Meredith almost never called me Ollie. "Did something go wrong again at school today?"

"Something's been going wrong at school since the beginning of last month when fifth grade started," I shot back. "Only I'm not going to discuss it with *you*. Because I know whose side you're on."

Merrie brought the macaroni casserole to the table between two pot holders and set it down carefully. "I honestly do not know what you're talking about. Do you intend to discuss this problem with anybody?"

"Yes," I said. "I intend to discuss it with my parents. When they get back. For heaven's sake, Merrie, do you know sometimes you sound . . . why, you even *look* like Miss Edith Marie Kilhenny."

Meredith gave me a chilly look and passed the

salad. "So, in addition to having to make up all the college work that she missed this week, Mom's going to have to deal with your running battle with a teacher you've simply made up your mind to dislike."

"That's your version of it," I said, making a face. I brushed a few ragged pieces of lettuce and some squooshy tomato onto my plate. "Okay, okay. I do feel bad about having to bother Mom with it. I know she's going to have her hands full when she gets home, what with bringing Uncle Russell back, getting his room fixed up, showing him the ropes, and all that."

Meredith looked up. "Oh, didn't I mention it? When Mom phoned last night—after you had talked to her and stomped off to your room, and when I got back on the wire—she told me that some cousins who live just outside Jacksonville have offered to take Uncle Russell to live with them. And Pop agreed. Because it seemed a much better idea than bringing him up north, changing his environment. People like that get very disoriented when you move them from place to place, you know."

My fork stopped in midair, dripping strands of cheese-sauced macaroni. I pointed it at Meredith. "Aha! That's why you're feeling so much better today. As long as you get your way, everything's dandy, isn't it?"

"Oh, come on, Olivia." She began to get very busy

with her food. "You know that's nonsense. The whole idea of his coming to live with us was ridiculous. Just when Mom's starting to find herself, becoming a person in her own right instead of just a . . . a housemaid and a kitchen slave."

"Oh, *please*," I exploded, getting really annoyed with Meredith. "Why don't you stop trying to feed me that pap? Now that you're safe from Uncle Russell, why don't you tell me the real reason you were so dead set against his coming here to live?"

Meredith's lip curled. "There is no 'real' reason aside from what I've already told you. If you're suddenly so smart, maybe you can tell *me* what it is."

I threw my fork down onto my plate. "I sure can," I sputtered. "The real reason is that you're the world's biggest snob, and you're afraid that your friends will lose their respect for you if they find out that you have a 'half-wit' relative—as you called him. Well, if you and your crowd of poetry-writing geniuses were really intelligent, you'd know that whatever's wrong with Uncle Russell isn't necessarily inherited and it certainly isn't catching, and you'd also be grown up enough to accept the fact that he's still a human being and somebody's got to give him a home."

Meredith had gone right on eating during most of my outburst. I guess she was feeling too good about Uncle Russell's *not* coming to have a fight with me about it, especially when I was already in a bad mood and Mom and Pop weren't home. She looked up at me calmly. "I really don't want to discuss it, Olivia. As I told you before, my main concern in this is Mom."

"All right," I went on, poking a few shreds of lettuce into my mouth and trying to match Meredith's cool, "let's talk about Mom then. I still don't see what was wrong with her the way she was. I think she's been doing a very good job of being a mom. And I don't think that's easy either. It probably takes real talent. But the way you've been pushing her lately, telling her she has to *be* something—it's like you don't think she's been *anything* up to now. I think that's insulting."

"Well, it's not meant to be at all," Meredith replied. "I've only been trying to open her eyes to the possibilities. She's got lots of years ahead of her that she could make good use of now that her family's growing up."

I shook my head. "I think Mom's smart enough to find out for herself what she wants to do when her family grows up. And I still think you're pushing her, shaming her even. It reminds me of what Kilhenny's trying to do to *me*."

The phone rang. Merrie gave me a quick look and jumped up to answer it. It was Mom.

"Where are you calling from?" Merrie asked in a

127

rush. "Are you at the airport?" Pause. "Oh, I see. Tomorrow then. Yes, she's fine. She's right here. And Greg phoned last night. He's fine, too. I told him you'd phone him when you got back. Do you want to talk to Olivia?"

I waved my hand at Merrie and shook my head no. I wasn't sure I could trust myself not to let on about all the mess at school.

"She has nothing special to say," Merrie told Mom. "Anyhow we'll see you tomorrow. Yes, we're really getting along fine. We're both fine. I'm telling you. Macaroni and cheese. And a salad." Another pause. "Cake and ice cream. There's still lots of stuff in the freezer. Don't worry about us. Okay, I will. Tomorrow then. Love to Dad. Bye. Bye-bye."

Merrie clicked the receiver onto the hook. "Some last-minute things Pop had to attend to down there. They couldn't make it today. They'll be home tomorrow."

"Yes," I said, putting down my fork and resting my chin in my hand. "I heard. Tomorrow."

11

Going to school the next morning was out of the
question. Besides, I had a good excuse. My mother
wasn't back yet and wouldn't be able to see Miss
Kilhenny that afternoon. But just to avoid having a
further discussion with Meredith, I got up early,
dressed, took my school books, and went over to
Anita's to call for her as usual.

Grandma Castellani came to the door smiling and
chirping at me as she always did, and ushered me
into the breakfast room. "Come inside. Sit a minute.
'Ere's Helen. She like a see you."

Ever since last Sunday when I'd told Anita about
my Uncle Russell, I'd noticed that Anita's Aunt
Helen had been allowed to hover around the front
hall in the mornings. Today the little pug-nosed per-

son was seated at the breakfast table drinking what looked like milky coffee out of a cereal bowl, which she was grasping between the short, stubby fingers of both hands. She was still too shy to say anything to me, but she smiled and bobbed her head several times until I finally sat down at the table opposite her. She acted so much like a little girl, a baby sister to Anita, that it was hard to think of her as being Anita's aunt (like Aunt Bea at the Beauty Boo-Teek), much less as Grandma Castellani's daughter. Grandma looked to be at least seventy.

Anita came clattering into the kitchen in new shoes, fastening her watch to her wrist. She had washed her hair the night before and its dark mass was full and curly with satiny highlights. She was wearing a flower-print blouse with a soft apricot-color sweater, not too tight of course.
I'd never seen her look prettier.

"You're early," she said, in a flat tone, sitting down next to her Aunt Helen. "Did you have your breakfast 'n' everything already?"

I shrugged. "I wasn't hungry this morning."

Anita passed me a plate of dry Italian toast that looked like zwieback. "Have some. It won't make you sick. I should know. It's practically the only thing I'll eat on school days." She glanced at Helen who was giggling delightedly since I'd bitten into the dry crumbly toast and started munching on it. "Look at her," Anita remarked. "She's happy you're eating with us. Now she's taking a piece of it. She's such a copycat. Whatever anybody else does, she does. All the time like that."

"Listen, Anita," I said, gulping down a chewed-up mouthful, "I'm not going to school with you today. I only came over here so I wouldn't have to explain things to my sister this morning. As soon as she leaves the house, around nine, I'm going back home." And I told her about my parents not returning home until some time later today. I didn't say anything about Merrie's news that Uncle Russell wasn't coming to live with us after all. Somehow, with Anita and her family being so much more open now about her Aunt Helen, that seemed like a kind of betrayal.

Anita nodded in understanding. "Yeah, I see how it is. You must feel awful after yesterday. Having your seat changed and all. Why does that Myrna Crossen hate you so?"

I waved an arm. "Oh, that's only a small part of it. Did you ever notice how when one thing goes wrong, everything starts to go wrong? Well, that's how it's been for me lately. Bad to worse, worse to worser. I don't know where it's going to end."

Helen's eyes had remained fixed on me the whole time. Her little mouth was somber now and her nose was running. Maybe it was from the hot coffee in the cereal bowl. I leaned across the table and rested my hand on her short chubby arm. "I'm okay," I told her. "You're not worrying about me, are you?"

She pitched her head forward and burst into an explosion of happy giggles. Grandma Castellani came over to my chair and patted my shoulder. "She no understand. You listen a Gran-mama. Your Mama no come back, you no go a school today, you stay 'ere. Stay. It's okay."

I shook my head. "No, everything's all right. Thanks anyway." I stood up and got my school books together. "Whenever you're ready, Anita," I said. "I'll walk you part of the way, anyhow."

We left the house with the usual shower of good-byes and good wishes from Gran-mama, and I trudged about four blocks toward the school with Anita. Finally, I stopped at the corner and told her I was going back.

"So what should I tell Miss Kilhenny?" she asked me, squinting into the slanting morning sun.

"Tell her . . . tell her to go fly a balloon to the moon. Tell her . . . Oh, don't tell her anything. When she calls the roll, she'll find out I'm absent."

Anita lifted her hand and waggled good-bye to me with two fingers. "Okay, Olivia. I hope things turn out all right. I'll phone you right after school."

I started walking back very slowly toward home. Meredith wouldn't be gone yet. When she did leave, though, she'd be going in the opposite direction, to catch the bus for high school, so at least there wasn't any danger of running into her. As I reached the block before ours, the block Buzz's house was on, I began to wonder if Buzz was staying home from school again today. I hadn't seen him this morning, although sometimes he took a different route. Since I didn't have anything else to do and plenty of time to kill, I decided I'd ring his bell. Just in case he *was* home.

I knew that Mrs. Delaney didn't like anybody to use the front door because it opened directly into "the parlor," as she called the living room, and she always said she didn't want her "best room to get all tracked up." So I headed for the side entrance.

The house had a long, straight, narrow driveway that led to the garage at the very back of the lot. The garage door was open and the garage was empty, which meant that Mrs. Delaney had already left for her job at the Super Bee. The other side of the driveway was bordered by a tall, dark hedge. It belonged to the Mullers, the elderly couple who lived next door in a neat brick house with a perfect front lawn and a row of well-manicured evergreen shrubs.

I went up the three steep steps of the narrow brick stoop that led to the Delaneys' side door and pressed the bell. No answer. After waiting a while, I tried again. Maybe Buzz was still sleeping. Or maybe he was sick in bed and couldn't come to the door. I tried the bell one more time. I could hear it ringing inside the house. Still no answer. So I went down the steps and farther on up the driveway, picked up a couple of bits of gravel, and tossed them lightly at Buzz's window. I waited and watched the window. Nothing.

It was now about five minutes to nine, and quiet and peaceful all through the neighborhood. Most of the people who went to work or to school every day had already left, and the people who stayed at home were probably just sitting down to a second cup of coffee, or making the beds, or dusting, or running their washing machines. I strolled around behind the Delaneys' screened back porch, which I had a view of from the window of my room. Close up, I saw that a lot of the screens were torn, and the furniture on the porch was sagging and faded and rain-spotted. The back garden was a mess, too, and so was the garage except for the empty space in the middle where Mrs. Delaney kept her car. No wonder the Mullers complained every now and then to the other neighbors about "that pigsty next door." But of course Mrs. Delaney worked and had nobody who could really help her to keep the place tidy.

At last my watch read nine o'clock and I decided it was probably safe to start for home. I got my books from the ledge of the screened porch where I'd parked them and was just about to start down the

Delaney driveway when I heard the softest possible crunching sound coming *up* the driveway from the street. Maybe it was Mr. Muller coming over to see who'd been tossing gravel at Buzz's window. I was a little embarrassed at being found there, so I stepped back behind the house and peeked out cautiously.

It wasn't stout, powdery-haired Mr. Muller at all. The person walking up the drive toward the side entrance of the Delaney house was a tall blond young man, dressed in ordinary jeans and a white tee shirt. At first he didn't look familiar at all and then, in a flash, I recognized him. I should have, because I'd seen him only about a week ago in the Delaneys' backyard. It was Harvey Epping.

I immediately had the terrible thought that maybe *Norman* was inside the house. Since he and Harvey were so inseparable, I was almost sure now that it must have been Harvey who was at the wheel of the car that Hughie had seen driving into the warehouse last Wednesday. And I also suspected that Harvey had been the "tall blond guy" Anita had spotted at Pop's gas station on Thursday, getting into the station wagon that had her father's stolen license plates on it. If only I'd been quick enough to get a good look at him that day. But I'd missed him. Anyhow, whatever Harvey was doing around here this morning, there was something about it I didn't like one bit.

Of course, there wasn't anything to stop me right

then and there from marching down the driveway and telling Harvey (if he asked me) that I'd been calling for Buzz who didn't seem to be home. But then how would I ever find out what Harvey was really up to?

So instead I just stayed hidden at the back of the house and kept watching. First, after mounting the stoop, Harvey rang the bell several times in rapid succession, like the gas man usually did when he came to read the meter. After that, Harvey began trying the doorknob, twisting it this way and that, even kicking his knee experimentally against the door once or twice. Then the phone started ringing in the kitchen. Was that why Harvey kept trying to peer through the curtained panes of glass in the upper part of the door? To see if anybody came to answer the phone?

Finally, the phone stopped ringing and I wished that Harvey would either break into the house (if that was what he was planning to do) or just go away. Because as things were, I was really trapped. On the other side of the Delaney house was a narrow strip of brambles and tall weeds with a cyclone fence tight up against it. The fence belonged to the neighbors over on that side, and enclosed not only their driveway but their entire property on all four sides. And I couldn't get to my own backyard—which was so near and yet so far—because Pop had a six-foot-tall solid redwood fence running across the rear of our garden. So I was very relieved when, after about five more minutes, which felt like five hours, Harvey began sauntering down the driveway toward the street. At least it didn't seem like Norman was in the house. In fact, it was pretty definite by now that nobody was in the Delaney house.

I figured I'd have to give Harvey time to get part of the way down the block before I made my escape. So I watched him turn to the left and disappear, counted impatiently to twenty, and started down the driveway when, suddenly ... there he was again! This time, he was standing in front of the driveway, facing the street, his hands locked behind his back, looking up and down the block in both directions as though he were waiting for someone.

I made a fast retreat up the driveway. But I was so scared that he might turn any minute and see me that I ducked behind the first thing I came to, which was the brick wall that formed the back of the side stoop. If I crouched real low behind it, he probably wouldn't be able to spot me even if he came up onto the stoop and started ringing the bell or trying the door again.

I was breathing hard and I didn't know how long I could remain in that awkward crouch, holding my books in my arms. In fact, I had just begun thinking of trying to make a run for the back of the house when I heard voices approaching, and footsteps—surely two pairs this time—crunching up the drive. As quickly as I could, I shifted my books to the ground, sat down on top of them with my back against the wall . . . and froze.

Just in time, too. The footsteps were right behind me now, mounting the stoop, and the voices were practically overhead. I could hear the faint jangle of keys.

"Don't *worry*, Norm baby," the first voice was saying. "Like I told you, it's all clear. Your old lady's at work, the kid went to school today for sure, and the money's layin' in the deep freeze. Now let's go get it, like you promised. Or Harvey's gonna spill a whole lot of beans."

"Okay, okay," the other voice whispered irritably. "Just take it easy, Harve." I could hear the sound of a key being softly fitted into the door lock. "We got lots of nosey neighbors," Norm's voice went on. "Did you case the backyard?"

"Nah, what for? I could see into the kitchen when the phone rang. Nobody answered it. That's a good trick, callin' first from a booth. I like it. What's with the key? Don't it work?"

"I don't know." There was a grunting sound. "Seems funny. Maybe she changed the damned lock. Lemme try a coupla others I got here. Hey, go case the back meanwhile. My kid brother could be out there messin' around in the yard. Anything."

"Awright," Harvey hissed back grouchily. "Only get that damned door open. And fast! I don't like hangin' around here anymore'n you do."

Harvey's shoes scrunched lightly down the steps and his body swung around toward the garage. Instinctively, I dipped my head and covered my eyes with my hands. But of course Harve Epping would have had to be blind not to see me.

"For cryin' out loud!" he exploded, forgetting how quiet he and Norman were trying to be.

I glanced up to see Harve towering above me, his hands on his hips and his small mouth stretched into a mean, unhappy grin.

"Hey, Norm," he growled, "take a look. Now what in hell are we gonna do with *this*?"

12

My first impulse was to try to get to my feet. But Harvey Epping pushed back hard at my shoulder and I tumbled into a heap on top of my books. I could see now why I hadn't recognized him at first. He was raising a small, pale-blond moustache and beard. The moustache looked like a smudge under his nose and the beard made his mouth look smaller and his chin pointier.

Norman Delaney was standing beside him, the bunch of keys dangling from his fingers.

"Who's this kid, anyway?" Harve demanded. He turned his greenish eyes on me. "Who are ya, kid?"

I felt terrified, too choked to answer. I couldn't believe how scared I was. My mouth had gone completely dry. The syllables of my name just wouldn't come out.

"Take it easy, Harve," Norman said, looking down at me with a serious expression. Norm wasn't red-haired and freckled like his kid brother, Buzz. He had dark, curly hair and smooth, neat features, with surprisingly red lips and rosy spots of color high on his cheeks. Actually he was sort of baby-faced except for his eyes which were narrow and slitted. "I think I know who she is. You're one of the Potts kids from around the block, aren't you?"

"R-r-right," I replied gratefully, pointing toward the back of the Delaney property. "We live r-r-right behind you. You even know my brother. From high school. Greg Potts. You both know him. I'm sure you do."

"Oh, yeah," Harve said slowly, scratching his ear. "I remember that guy Potts. Big brain, wasn't he? Even in junior high. Number one everything. School hero."

I nodded eagerly. "He even won a scholarship to Yale. That's where he is now. Yale."

Harve turned and poked Norman in the ribs with his elbow. "Yeah. Big deal," he grinned. His hands returned to his hips and he bent forward a little. "So okay, kid. Very nice and all that. But see, that don't explain a thing about what you were doin' sneakin' around here. This here's Norm's place, you know."

"I wasn't sneaking around," I objected. "Listen, can't I get up? It's very uncomfortable sitting here, and you hurt me, you know, when you pushed me down just now." I began trying to get to my feet. But Harvey's big hand, palm out, shot toward me again.

To my relief, Norm grabbed it and pushed it aside. "Let her up," he said softly. "She ain't goin' nowhere."

I looked up at Norm in worried shock. Up to now, I'd thought he was on my side, at least willing to give me a chance. I stood up shakily, stumbling on a couple of my school books and kicking them out of the way. But now I felt even more cornered than before. I was wedged into the spot where the stucco wall of the house and the brick wall of the side stoop came together at a right angle. The figures of Norman and Harvey had me completely blocked in. Harve was taller than Norm, and naturally they were both much taller than I was.

"So okay, let's have some answers now and quick," Norm ordered, extending one hand past my head and resting it on the railing of the stoop, hemming me in on that side. "Like my friend says, tell us what you were doing here."

"Yeah," Harve chimed in, "and what you heard."

Norman gave Harvey a shove with his other hand, indicating for him to shut up.

"I wasn't doing anything at all," I replied, trying hard to keep my voice from breaking. "I came to call for Buzz. We're in the same class. You probably know that. I thought we'd walk to school together."

Norm glanced at his wristwatch. "Yeah, well it's a little late for school, don't you think? I happen to know Buzz leaves here around eight-fifteen. So if you're in the same class as him, you oughta know that, too."

"I know," I said, licking my lips and thinking hard. "But see, I overslept and . . . and my clock stopped . . . and I thought maybe I'd still catch him. Only I guess I was too late. I must have missed him."

"Yeah," Harvey agreed sourly. "By about forty-five minutes at least. That's a lousy story. So if you missed him, what were you hangin' around here for?"

"Well, see, I . . . I didn't want to go to school much this morning anyway. I got into trouble with my teacher yesterday and she told me that my mother should come to see her. But my mother doesn't know about it yet." I looked at them both imploringly. "It's true. It's really true. We have this awful teacher and she's been riding me ever since school started. You can ask Buzz. Anybody. They'll tell you. Killer Henny. That's what Buzz and everyone else calls her."

"So you ain't brainy like your big brother, huh?" Harve chortled. "You're one of those dumb kids who's always gettin' into trouble."

"Right," I said. "I guess I'm just dumb." I was

almost going to add, "Like you and Norman were in school." But instead I said, "Lots of kids are that way in school. Dumb, you know."

Harve's smile died. "Okay, dummy. So let's say you didn't want to go to school today and you didn't want to go home and get yelled at. So you were hangin' out here, sittin' behind the stoop. Which I don't buy." He poked Norman. "You don't buy it either, Norm, do you?"

Norm shook his head. "Nope, I don't buy it either."

A flicker of terror ran through me. "So now," Harve said, thickening his voice into a fierce whisper, "what did you *hear*?"

I looked from one to the other, stunned. "Nothing."

Harve reached out slowly, then suddenly grabbed my shoulders and started shaking me. "What did you hear us say? We was talkin' up there on the stoop. Sayin' WORDS. Now what words did we say?"

I tried shaking my head rapidly back and forth to deny I'd heard anything, but of course I couldn't because Harvey's fingers were digging into my skin now and he was shaking me so furiously that my head bounced with a hard crack against the wall of the house. The knock made Harvey release his grip and, at the same time, sent an enormous shudder through me which seemed to release me from the numbing fear that had enveloped me from the first moment that Harvey had discovered me hiding there.

"Nothing!" I screamed out at the top of my lungs. "Nothing, *nothing*, NOTHING!" And with that I dashed along the brick wall, ducked out from under Norman's arm, and headed for the driveway and the street beyond. Why hadn't I screamed before? Surely somebody would hear me. The Mullers certainly ought to, because they were the closest. Somebody, anybody. Besides it felt good. And the more I screamed, the more I wanted to scream. In fact, I wasn't sure I could ever stop screaming, except . . .

Except that a hand was suddenly clapped over my mouth, an arm was clamped tightly around my neck, my feet were being lifted off the ground, and the next moment I was being carried, kicking and gagging, toward the empty Delaney garage.

I heard grunts and groans and curses all around me. I couldn't make out which were coming from Norman and which from Harvey, or who was actually carrying me, or who had just put a fist in my mouth (which I was trying hard to bite), or which one was now panting to the other, "This lousy kid. We gotta get rid of her. Shut her up once and for all. Drop her! C'mon, we gotta get outa here. There, there. That's good. C'mon now, let's go."

I was dropped hard onto a pile of junk in the dim

rear of the Delaney garage. In the shadowy light I could make out a sled with rusty runners, heaps of old auto parts and broken gardening tools, all sorts of sharp-edged metal garbage. And the thing that I seemed to be sitting on, or rather *in*, was the fire pit of a greasy, blackened, round barbecue grill. I was screaming hard again now, no words, just uncontrollable roars from deep inside my throat. My hair was in my eyes, angry tears were streaking my vision, my glasses were knocked crooked, and all I could see as I looked toward the light were the wildly running figures of Norman and Harvey racing toward the doorway of the garage, reaching up for the overhead handles, and pulling the big door down smack to the ground in one giant slam!

Total blackness. I was horrified at how dark it was. I blinked rapidly hoping it had only been a trick of my eyes. How quiet it was, too. I'd stopped screaming. It seemed useless now.

The main thing I wanted was to get myself out of the pit of the barbecue grill. I felt like somebody who'd fallen into a toilet bowl that was about three feet off the ground. My legs were no help at all. All I could do was push hard against the rough, grease-caked metal rim of the grill with my hands and arms, and try to raise the upper part of my body so I could jump off.

Finally, after a few tries, I succeeded and landed in the surrounding heap of metal junk, getting jabbed and scratched in a number of places. I just hated Mrs. Delaney for keeping such a mess and never tidying anything up. From now on, I was on Mr. Muller's side.

I didn't have anything with me, not even a hanky or a tissue. My books, my purse, were all out in the driveway. Unless, of course, Norm and Harvey had taken my purse, which had my lunch money and some extra allowance money in it. Where had they run off to now, I wondered, and would the police ever catch up with them? I choked back a couple of sobs, wiped my glasses on my blouse and my eyes on my sleeve, and tried to put the terrible experience out of my mind.

I was beginning to make out shapes now in the garage, and I could see a long, knife-thin slit of light coming from the bottom of the garage door where it met the ground. I guess the first thing any prisoner does after being locked up is to go over and try the bars. Well, I did, and of course my "cell bars"—the door—wouldn't budge. It was locked all right. And I was trapped.

For how long, I wondered? I figured Mrs. Delaney would be coming home from the supermarket around six. Maybe five, if I was lucky. It was now only around half-past nine in the morning. I'd

147

starve. I'd suffocate from lack of air and from breathing the awful, stale oil-and-gas fumes of the closed garage. I'd go stark raving mad from all those long hours in solitary. I began to sob again, my head and arms pressed against the garage door.

After a while, an idea came to me. I lay down on the floor alongside the door and tried calling for help through the slit. Surely somebody would be passing by in the street, surely the Mullers couldn't be *that* deaf. But my "helps" sounded empty and ridiculous even to me. They grew weaker and weaker and, at last, I stopped altogether. I sat up, leaning my back against the garage door, and tried hard to think.

The first thing I told myself was not to panic. Wasn't that what they always told people who were trapped in elevators? And the Delaney garage, horrible though it was, was still better than a stuck elevator. It couldn't drop down to some sub-basement and smash to bits, since it was already on the ground. Then, too, it was bigger, it was lighter, it was roomier, and it was probably even airier. Also, if help ever came, I wouldn't have to climb out through the top, crawl onto a ledge, or jump twelve feet to the floor below. All I'd have to do would be to step out into the Delaney driveway and walk around the block to my own house. *If* help ever came. . .

As I was thinking all this, another thought struck me. Suppose Norman and Harvey decided to sneak back and set the garage on fire, bomb it, blow it to bits, in order to destroy the evidence inside, namely *me*. Because I really had found out what they were up to. Which was why they had locked me in here, kicking and screaming, in the first place.

They had come to steal money from Norman's mother's deep freeze. The *deep freeze*? Did Mrs. Delaney really keep money in her freezer? I guess so. And why not? It sounded like a pretty good place. Safe from fire, too. I remembered now that I'd once heard about a lady who kept her diamond rings in a jar of instant coffee in the refrigerator. Then there were people who kept jewelry in the bottoms of their sugar bowls. How about in a box of oatmeal or Wheaties? Working in a supermarket could give you lots of ideas. Until of course the crooks found out about it, which they always did, it seemed, in the end.

I leaned my head back against the garage door and wondered what the real end was going to be. Not just for Norman and Harvey, those two rotten, no-good, lunkheaded partners-in-crime. What about the end for me? What about Miss Kilhenny and fifth grade? What about walking into that classroom again and having to take my seat in the front row where Miss Kilhenny could "keep an eye" on me. What about those ugly, staring looks from

Myrna Crossen and Zelda Barton, and those smirking glances from the rest of the class, to say nothing of the frosty disapproval of my brainy sister, Meredith.

Then there was Mom, helplessly throwing up her hands and saying how impossible it was that one of *her* children should ever have trouble at school. And there was Pop laughing in good-natured admiration at my joke about the Potts' brain chain. Maybe if Mom and Pop *had* brought Uncle Russell to live with us, they'd have realized that there were a couple of weak links in that chain. Uncle Russell was one of them. Wasn't it just possible that I was another?

Look at Anita, for example. In her family, there was her Aunt Helen. Maybe Mongolism wasn't supposed to be inherited, but I'd noticed that Anita's mother had made sure to have only one child. And Anita herself, while she was far from dumb in lots of ways, wasn't what you would call smart at school. If I *was* dumb, why couldn't I be left alone to be quietly, calmly, and contentedly dumb. And if I wasn't dumb, why couldn't I be left alone to discover and decide what I liked to do best and what I wanted to be smart *at*. It wasn't as if I hadn't been keeping up with most of the class in first, second, third, and fourth grades. It was just that Miss Kilhenny insisted that I should leap way out in front in fifth grade. For whose good? Hers or mine?

My head was beginning to flop forward and I realized how tired I was. I'd gotten up extra early that morning after a restless night full of bad dreams, I hadn't eaten anything for breakfast except a piece of cold, dry, licorice-tasting Italian toast, without butter, and I was exhausted from being scared and screaming hard and thinking until I was dizzy and droopy. And awfully drowsy, too. . . .

Somebody was kicking me in the back. I woke up with a start. I was still alone inside the dark garage, partly leaning against the door and partly sprawled out on the floor. A couple of more bangs struck near the base of my spine. I scrambled to my feet. Someone was pounding hard on the outside of the garage door. Then there was a voice, very close to my ear and only slightly muffled by the door between.

"Oh, I'll whip that boy, I will. Closin' the garage door on me when he knows I never bother with closin' it anymore. Oh, I *can't* find the right key." It was Mrs. Delaney for sure, muttering irritably to herself. "Well, never mind. There isn't anything in there I need just now anyway." The voice was beginning to drift off.

I quickly came to my senses and banged back hard at the door. "Mrs. Delaney!" I yelled as loudly as I could. "MISSUS DELANEY. Come back! Let me out of here. You've *got* to get someone to open this door. Or I'll be in here *forever*."

It wasn't an exaggeration. With the slipshod way Buzz's mother did things, she might not get around to finding the right key for the garage until the first snow, or Christmas—whichever came first—when maybe, just maybe, Buzz would want his sled with the rusty runners. Meanwhile, it took only forty-eight hours without water to die, and if it was now six o'clock in the evening, I already had a lot less than two days to live!

So I kept up the screaming and yelling and pounding, praying that Mrs. Delaney could hear me from inside the house, that she hadn't gone off again with the car, that the Mullers would *please* turn their hearing aids up, that somebody, *anybody*, would come to rescue me before it was too late.

13

There was a soft, insistent tapping on the garage door.

I stopped shrieking and banging for a few moments and listened.

"Who's in there?" a soft, husky man's voice called.

"Who's *that*?" I asked suspiciously. I wanted to be freed, but not into the clutches of Norman or Harvey or some other criminal type.

"Just calm down and we'll have you out of there in no time," the voice continued. "Now say who you are and what kind of mischief you've been up to."

"Mischief!" I called back indignantly. "I was locked up in here kicking and screaming by . . . Wait a minute. Who *are* you, anyway?"

"I'm Ernest Muller, young lady, from just the next

house. Now, Mrs. Delaney's gone to rummage through her keys to try to find the one that fits the garage lock and if she can't, why, I've got a tool here that'll have you out of there in a jiffy. So just hold on a little while longer. . . ."

I slammed my hands repeatedly against the garage door, like a prisoner who was about to be released impatiently rattling the cell bars. "Oh, Mr. Muller," I cried out with rising hysteria, "it's Olivia Potts from around the corner. Where *were* you all this time? Why couldn't you *hear* me?"

I was seated at Mrs. Muller's kitchen table eating a bowl of thick, steaming hot, split-pea soup. To my great surprise, it was only lunchtime. I had been locked in the Delaney garage just a little over two hours. But it felt more like an entire day.

"What a piece of luck," Mrs. Delaney had exclaimed when Mr. Muller finally got me out, "that I came home for a bit of lunch and a lie-down. Oh, I told them I'd be happy to make up the time in the evening shift. I just had to rest my aching back."

Needless to say, Mrs. Delaney hadn't been able to find the garage-door key, and Mr. Muller had finally sheared through the lock with his electric power saw.

Nor did I get much of a chance to explain to Mrs. Delaney and Mr. Muller how I'd gotten locked up in the garage in the first place. Nor did Mrs. Delaney ever get her lie-down. I was still blinking in the unexpected brightness of the October noon sunshine that flooded the Delaney driveway, when the police phoned Mrs. Delaney to ask her to come down to the station and identify her son Norman. He and Harvey had been caught stealing a car and were at the precinct house being booked. Charges were being pressed by the car's owner, and Norm was in bad trouble.

Poor Mrs. Delaney had crumpled at the telephone and Mr. Muller ran in at the sound of her hoarse screeches and offered to drive her to the police station. By that time, Mrs. Muller had hurried out to the Delaney driveway and was bundling me off to her house for "a good wash, a hot meal, and a rest."

Mrs. Muller was small and shrunken, with a hunched-over body and a deeply wrinkled face with a stern expression. She looked older than her husband, probably because he was healthily stout-looking and had a large, smooth face, although there were a couple of chins hanging from it. Mrs. Muller was very kind and gentle to me, and I was sorry now that I'd never known her better. I'd once thrown rotten apples on her lawn because Meredith and Gregory had told me to. The Mullers' house was on the corner and they used to yell at the kids from our block for cutting across their garden on the way to elementary school. Soon all the kids, big and small,

155

were in a campaign against them, annoying them in all sorts of mean and stupid little ways. It went on for a couple of years and it was really dumb.

"You see, it was our grocery-shopping morning, dear," Mrs. Muller explained, reaching up to put some canned goods away in a cupboard, while I spooned up the delicious hot soup. "We always go on Thursdays, after the Wednesday food ads and the food coupons appear in the papers. And Ernst," she didn't call him Ernest, "likes to get there when the doors open. Most any other day, we'd surely have been home and heard your cries. Imagine those two big hooligans bullying you and terrifying you like that. Why you might have been very badly hurt."

Mrs. Muller came over and ladled some more soup into my bowl and put a glass of milk and two big thick jelly doughnuts down beside me.

"I don't know what will happen now," she sighed. "Tell you the truth, Ernst and I were very relieved when that boy disappeared from the neighborhood and his mother told me he was off working someplace down south. He himself was fairly quiet, though a little sneaky-looking, but I never liked those friends he used to bring around here. Hooligans, all of 'em."

Tiny Mrs. Muller dug deep into one of the grocery bags and came up triumphantly with a whole smoked ham. "But to *think* that Norman Delaney would actually wind up trying to steal cars and burglarize houses—his own mother's even! Well, we'd none of us be safe around here."

I spent most of the afternoon sleeping in a big old-fashioned double bed in Mrs. Muller's guest room, after making her promise that she'd keep phoning my house every half-hour to see if Mom and Pop had arrived home yet. She had insisted that she wouldn't let me go back there alone, no matter what.

By three-thirty when Buzz came home from school, there was still no answer. Mrs. Muller, who was watching for Buzz from her window, called him inside and told him not to go to the supermarket today.

"But it's Thursday," Buzz told her excitedly. "There'll be lots of packages to carry to the cars. It's my best day, next to Friday and Saturday." Then he saw me just coming out of Mrs. Muller's guest bedroom, rubbing my eyes, and he became completely bewildered.

"Hey, what the . . .? What are *you* doin' here?"

"Mrs. Muller's taking care of all us stray kids today," I answered, trying to keep my voice light and humorous. "Come on in and join the club."

It was Saturday morning.

"Mom, honestly, can't I get up today? It's nice being a wounded hero—or heroine—or whatever, but I'm going to get *sick* from resting in bed so much."

Mom had come into my room very quietly so as not to wake me if I was still asleep. Poor Mom—she looked like *she* hadn't had any sleep for a week, and probably she hadn't. Between the emergency trip to Florida and the funeral, the awful news about me when she and Pop had returned Thursday evening and brought me home from Mrs. Muller's house, and Mom's efforts to catch up on her reading for the three nights of college classes she'd missed, it was no wonder she could barely stand on her feet and had deep, dark circles under her eyes.

"Maybe you're the one who ought to be in bed," I suggested to Mom as I threw off the covers. "You look all dragged out."

Mom sagged down onto the edge of the bed. "I am," she said with a wan smile. "You know, Ollie, I feel every bit my age this week. Maybe 'life begins at forty' isn't such a good idea after all. Merrie seems to think it's the right time for me to start a new life by going off to college. But I haven't exactly gotten rid of my old life. And carrying on *two* lives . . . Well . . ." Mom shook her head from side to side letting her hair bounce all over and fall into her eyes. "I just don't know about that. . . ."

I watched her without saying anything. Quickly she pulled herself together. "Anyhow, as for you, missy, yes, you may get up. In fact you'll also have to get dressed. You've got a visitor."

"Oh, I can see her this way." I glanced down indifferently at my rumpled flannel pajamas. Anita had been coming over to see me at least once a day since Thursday evening.

"Uh-uh, it's not a her," Mom said with a soft, rippling laugh. "It's a him."

"A him?" I swung my feet off the bed and pushed them into my slippers. "Who?"

"Someone from your class," Mom replied, "and I'll leave you to guess the rest."

I wondered if it could be Hughie Rand. Anita had been talking to me about him more and more in the last few days. It seems he had asked her if she was going to the Hamburger Barn for lunch again this Saturday. "I think he likes me," she'd said shyly. "He looks over at me a lot in class. And he's never called me 'Big B' since that first time, when you made such a fuss about it. Maybe he *thinks* it. But I can't help what's in his mind, can I?"

I speeded up in spite of the annoying bruises and scratches that I was still discovering all over me, and piled into a pair of jeans and a new long-sleeved lavender tee shirt with a painting of a big slice of lemon meringue pie sitting right in the middle of the front.

It wasn't Hughie who was waiting for me down in

the living room. It was Stevie Gould. I should have known. He was sitting very stiffly on the couch with a small package wrapped in striped, colored paper resting in his lap.

"Hi," he said, jumping off the couch with a startled look. "Are you okay, Olivia?"

"Sure," I said. "I hurt in a couple of places from getting pushed around, but I'm okay."

Stevie shoved the package into my hand and sat down again. "Gee, I'm relieved. I heard you were in pretty bad shape. We were all plenty worried about you when we got the news. You could have been hurt bad."

"Only if I hadn't gotten out of that garage in time." I glanced up at the clock on the living room wall. "I'd have been dead by now. Do you realize that? I would have gone forty-eight hours without water."

Stevie shook his head in sympathy. "Right. Dehydration. It's a real killer. Did I ever tell you that story about the guy who died of thirst in the desert sitting at the wheel of his car? He was only three feet away from a supply of water that could have kept him alive until help came, a couple of hours later. If only he'd had the brains to drink it. It was the water in his car radiator."

I nodded. Stevie had been telling me and everyone else that story since third grade. "What's this package for?" I asked, holding it up.

"It's for you," he answered, looking across the room instead of at me.

"From our class?" I asked, turning it over in my hands.

"No," he exclaimed almost angrily, still not looking in my direction. "From me."

"Why?" I sat down and started to open the package anxiously and rather clumsily, tearing across the pretty rose, green, and gold striped paper. Stevie still hadn't answered my question.

Inside was an oblong, white pasteboard box. I lifted the lid cautiously and peered into it. Resting on a layer of white cotton wool were loops upon loops of olive pits, laid end to end. Olive pits! I could feel a flush of anger spreading through my cheeks.

"Lift it up," Stevie said encouragingly. "It's beads. To wear around your neck. It would probably look very good with what you're wearing right now. Try it on."

I picked up the so-called beads by a single olive pit and saw that it really was a necklace. I probably had been too suspicious. The beads themselves weren't real olive pits. Actually they were made of wood carved into slim, pointed, oblong shapes. And between every two of the brown wooden beads there was a small round gold bead. The necklace was really very pretty. My cheeks got even hotter.

"It's all hand-carved, out of real olive wood," Stevie said shyly. "It comes from Spain. There was a tag on there that said so. It . . . it must have fallen into the box. Anyhow, that's why I got those beads for you. They sort of matched your name. Olivia. Get it?"

I slipped the necklace on over my head. It dangled just to the top of the crust of the lemon meringue pie. "Thank you very much, Stevie." I couldn't say any more. I never thought anything like this (whatever it was) would happen between Stevie, the math and science whiz, and me. There was an awkward silence.

"So listen," I said, jumping up and offering Stevie a hard candy from a dish that was sitting on the coffee table, "what's new at school?"

He sucked on the candy and leaned forward, dangling his hands between his knees. "What should be new? It's the same old routine. Anyhow, you only missed two days so far." He gave me a curious look. "When you coming back?"

I looked away. "Never, I hope."

"Be sensible. You can't do that, Olivia. You still have to finish fifth grade. And sixth grade . . ."

"And seventh, and eighth, and ninth, and finish high school, and go to college. And keep up all the way with the brainy Potts family." I sighed. "Well, to tell you the truth, it's all a big mess and I'd rather not talk about it just now."

We dropped the subject and talked about Norman

Delaney and Harvey Epping, which of course was what Stevie had come over to hear about.

"I found out a lot more about fences and set-ups, and all that stuff," he told me after a while. "Not just from my father. There are actually books in the library that tell you how burglars operate. You know, like confession stories written by guys who've gone to prison."

"Oh, really," I said with mild interest. "You already told me what a fence is. What's a set-up?"

Stevie leaned toward the coffee table and grabbed another candy. "That's a way of preparing for the crime by someone else who's really working with the thief. Setting it up, see? Like another person could distract your attention while the pickpocket takes your wallet. The first guy is the set-up. Or a burglar might find out when somebody's going to be away from home by getting a tip from a maid or handyman who's really working on his side. They're his set-up." He cracked the candy in half with his teeth and started crunching it.

"Sometimes people are their own set-up without realizing it," Stevie went on, all excited about his discoveries. "Say they put an announcement in the paper about a wedding or a funeral, or some other special occasion when they're going to be away from their house. Well, they're leaving themselves wide open. Oh, and even dumber is when they put a notice on a bulletin board in a neighborhood supermarket, or some other place near where they live, saying they have a diamond ring for sale or a high-priced stereo or something like that."

"Well," I broke in, "as far as Harvey and Norman went, I don't think they were bothering much about set-ups. It's no big deal to steal your own mother's brand-new color TV set. All you have to do is be mean enough."

Down at the police station, Norman had broken down completely and confessed everything. He'd come back north about ten days ago, after losing his job down south, and had stayed with his old pal, Harvey Epping, who had some secret plans about their "going into business together." Norman had phoned his mother from Harvey's, telling her he was still in Maryland, and she happened to mention the new TV set that was coming the next week.

So Norm had called the store and said Mrs. Delaney wanted them to deliver it on Wednesday morning. He'd let himself into the house with his key, forged his mother's signature to the store's delivery receipt, and then hauled the set off to the fence in the warehouse, in a station wagon that Harvey had stolen that morning.

Harvey had been afraid that once the stolen car was reported missing, the cops would trace it by its plates. So he'd immediately brought it over to Norman's garage, removed the plates, and replaced them with new plates, which he stole from Anita's father's car. Harvey had gotten into the Brunellis' driveway by squirming through the high, thick hedge at the back of the Mullers' property.

Not only that. Norman admitted that he'd stolen his mother's first color TV set, too, last summer! That was when he was still living at home, just before he took that job down south. The fence hadn't given him very much for that set because it was used, but he'd promised Norm plenty if he ever brought him a brand-new one. Who knows, now that the police had been led to the fence, maybe the "used furniture" warehouse would be pulled down and we'd finally get that new playground in its place. Meanwhile, Norm and Harve were waiting for their hearing before a judge, and nobody knew what was going to happen after that.

Stevie got up to leave. "Since you already had all those suspicions about Norm and Harvey, you were taking an awful chance, Olivia, hanging around there in Buzz's backyard after you saw Harvey arrive. You should have figured something was up and scooted out of there fast."

I fingered the lovely smooth beads of my olive-wood necklace. "Oh, I figured something was up," I assured Stevie. "That's why I decided to stay and spy on him. I just couldn't stand to . . . to not know the whole story of what was going on, when there was such a good chance to find out. That would have seemed so dumb."

Stevie scratched his head. "Yeah, well it's a question of which would have been dumber, to go or to stay. Maybe . . . maybe you also have to be dumb to be brave."

"Oh, thanks a heap," I said sarcastically.

Stevie turned. "No, really, I didn't mean that in a bad way, Olivia. I admire you."

I walked him to the door and thanked him again for the present he'd brought me. I wondered if he'd meant it in a bad way when he and Hughie had called Anita "Big B" and me "Olive Pits." But of course I couldn't ask him that. And, as Anita said, it was no use getting upset about what somebody might be *thinking*.

Just as he was about to go down the front steps, Stevie turned one more time. "By the way, Olivia, you still didn't tell me when you're coming back to class."

"How can I?" I replied, feeling a clutch of cold panic seize my chest beneath the warmth of the olive-wood beads. "I don't know myself. And I won't know anything until after my mother has her conference with Miss Kilhenny. Some day next week."

14

I felt like a first-grader getting ready to go to school
with Mom on Tuesday afternoon to see Miss Kilhenny. At first I was surprised that Miss Kilhenny
had told Mom on the phone that I should come to
the conference, too. Our appointment was for 3:15,
and Mom and I were both pretty nervous.

Mom hadn't asked me many questions about what
had gone wrong at school. She said she thought it
was fairer for Miss Kilhenny to give her side and for
me to give my side when we actually got together.

Miss Kilhenny was waiting for us at the door of
Room 324. She was wearing a dress of dark-purple
wool instead of her usual pale blue, dull beige, or
speckled gray, and had even applied the tiniest bit of
pale, pale pink lipstick to her lips.

"My dear Mrs. Potts," she said, actually smiling so her eyes crinkled slightly and taking Mom's hand in both of hers. "It's so *nice* to see you again." I guess Mom and Miss Kilhenny hadn't gotten together since Meredith was in sixth grade, and not for a reason anything like this.

We went into the empty classroom and sat down on chairs drawn up to Miss Kilhenny's desk. My old seat in front of Myrna Crossen's seemed to stare at me accusingly, while I glared uncomfortably at my new seat next to Zelda Barton's.

Miss Kilhenny was telling Mom how proud she was of Meredith's "literary achievements" and Gregory's "brilliant scholarship." It sounded to me like she was personally taking a generous heaping of the credit. She also told Mom how sorry she was to hear about the recent death in Pop's family and "worst of all, of Olivia's harrowing brush with the criminal world."

Then she turned her attention to me. "I'm glad to see you're looking quite recovered, Olivia. You survived what could have been a very serious situation."

I nodded and gulped.

"And when do you think you'll be ready to return to us, Olivia?"

"Us" meant Miss Kilhenny's fifth-grade class. I squirmed. "Well, I don't know. Anytime, I guess. Only . . ."

"Only?"

"Well," I looked from Miss Kilhenny to Mom, who was leaning forward slightly, listening intently, "it's like I said in my composition."

Mom turned to me. "What composition is that?"

"You haven't seen it?" Miss Kilhenny inquired. "All right, Mrs. Potts, that's a very good place to start. Last week I asked Olivia to write a composition for me entitled 'Why I Am Not Living Up to My Full Potential in Fifth Grade'." Miss Kilhenny pulled open her desk drawer, whipped out the large brown envelope marked PERSONAL, and handed it to Mom, who accepted it with a surprised and hesitant look.

Then Miss Kilhenny got up and went to the back of the room where she started busying herself at one of the cabinets. I sat quietly beside Mom while she read, staring numbly at the scarred surface of Miss Kilhenny's desk.

After what seemed like a very long time, Mom finished and softly laid the pages down on the corner of the desk.

"You were certainly very outspoken, Ollie," she said to me in a low voice. "You talk about all of us in those pages, about the whole family. You talk about . . . about me."

"I know," I said, still not looking up.

Mom brought her head closer. "I didn't know you

actually 'hated' my going to college. Why didn't you tell me?"

I shrugged. "It . . . it didn't bother me so much at first. But I guess it began annoying me more and more. Especially when I saw how you were getting carried away by Meredith's ideas and not paying any attention to mine."

"Oh, Ollie," Mom said in dismay. "I never meant it to appear like that. And is that what started you off having trouble at school?"

"Not only that," I admitted. "But I think it must have been part of it. I began to figure that if I was going to be the only dumb one left in the family, I might as well make a good job of it. After all, why not? Dumb is easier than smart."

Mom shook her head. "I'm still not sure what that's got to do with not doing the assignments Miss Kilhenny gave you. I'm sure you were smart enough to do the work."

Miss Kilhenny closed the cabinet door with a sharp click and started for the front of the room.

"I wrote it all in there," I whispered frantically to Mom, pointing to the pages lying on the desk. "She was always pushing me, putting me in competition with my brainy family and with all the smartest kids in fifth grade. I just had to push back."

Miss Kilhenny had returned to her desk. She sat down, smoothed her skirt, and looked inquiringly at

Mom. "Well, what do you think, Mrs. Potts? Did you know about Olivia's growing rebellion against the whole learning situation?"

"Not really," Mom replied. "I'm quite surprised, I confess. I can see now that my enrolling at college may be causing a number of family problems."

Miss Kilhenny leaned forward. "Oh, no, Mrs. Potts. You mustn't blame yourself. And you mustn't think of dropping your courses. You're doing an admirable thing. I'm sure Olivia will see it that way in time."

Miss Kilhenny leaned forward. "Oh, no, Mrs. Potts. "Now, as Olivia has probably told you, things did get a little out of hand last week and we ran into a small discipline problem, as a result of which I had to change Olivia's seat. I realize that was an embarrassment to her, so what I propose to do is to give her back her old seat when she returns to school, without any further discussion of the matter." Miss Kilhenny folded her hands on her desk and looked very pleased with her suggestion.

I swallowed hard and shook my head. Miss Kilhenny stared at me questioningly. "I don't want it back," I muttered in a hollow voice.

Miss Kilhenny's eyes opened wide in surprise. "You don't?"

"No. I don't want anything old back. I . . . I'd like to get a fresh start."

171

"Exactly right," Miss Kilhenny said with an air of relief. "That's precisely what we'll do, Olivia. Begin again as if nothing happened."

I shook my head even harder. "No. I don't think you see what I mean, Miss Kilhenny. I want a really fresh start. I want to be transferred to a different fifth-grade class."

Miss Kilhenny's mouth fell open. "What? Leave my class?"

I looked desperately at Mom. "I can, can't I? Why not?"

Mom didn't answer me. Her eyes remained fixed on Miss Kilhenny.

"I don't know," Miss Kilhenny said slowly, still trying to recover from the shock. "It's . . . it's a little unusual. Don't you think so, Mrs. Potts?"

Mom looked at me, her gaze firm and her large, soft, brown eyes very serious. "Are you sure that's what you really want, Ollie? Have you thought about it carefully?"

"Yes," I said. "It is. I've thought about it a lot. I don't like the idea of leaving some of my friends in this class. But it's what I really want."

Miss Kilhenny picked up a freshly sharpened pencil and tapped it against her desk. "I really don't see. . . ," she began. She put the pencil down abruptly. "Well, how do *you* feel about it, Mrs. Potts? Naturally you would have to make a formal request through the principal's office. And there would have to be room for a new student in one of the other classes. And the teacher of that class would have to be willing to take a transferee."

"You had to take Anita," I quickly reminded Miss Kilhenny. "Anita Brunelli, the new girl? If I left, then the class would be back to its normal size. That would make it easier to teach, wouldn't it?"

"It's a point," Miss Kilhenny remarked doubtfully. But I could see she was thinking that it might not make a bad excuse for her to give the class and the other fifth-grade teachers.

"Let's do it then," Mom said with sudden decisiveness. "Olivia's had an upsetting time so far this school year. The family upheaval because of my going off to college, that dreadful experience last week."

Miss Kilhenny looked at Mom searchingly. "You're sure now, Mrs. Potts. You're very sure you approve of this. Once Olivia is transferred out of my class, there'll be no reversing the process."

Mom nodded and turned to me. "We understand, don't we?"

"All right," Miss Kilhenny said, with an air of deep resignation. "I'll go along with you, Mrs. Potts. I just hope we're handling this the right way."

"I think we are," Mom said softly. "And I do appreciate your being so understanding about Olivia, Miss Kilhenny."

"Oh, I know Olivia," Miss Kilhenny assured Mom

with a confident air. "Perhaps the trouble has been that I know Olivia *too* well."

Mom and I got up to go, and I took a last look at the fifth-grade classroom that I wouldn't be coming back to. I'd especially miss Anita and Stevie, and even Hughie and Buzz Delaney. But the hours I spent in the classroom weren't my whole life. There were plenty of others besides. And, of course, I'd be making new friends in the class I'd be transferred to. As for Miss Kilhenny, I couldn't agree with what she'd just said about knowing me too well. I still felt she didn't know me well *enough*.

. Weeks have gone by and tomorrow is Thanksgiving, definitely my favorite holiday. I'm in Mr. Jenner's class now. I never knew a teacher could tell that many jokes and still give that many hard quizzes and tests. I like him so much, though (not only because he's young and funny-looking and teases us all so much), that I'd even do extra homework assignments for him. Only I'd never say that to anyone!

In addition to all the Thanksgiving dinner preparations, Merrie has just moved into my room. It's only for the weekend, though, because Greg is coming home for Thanksgiving and he's going to be using Meredith's room. The reason for that is that Uncle Russell is coming to live with us after all, and he's going to be moving into Gregory's room. In fact,

Pop's at the airport now meeting Russell's plane.

Mom told me about all this only last night.

"What happened?" I asked. "I thought those other relatives in Florida were taking care of Uncle Russell and everything was fine."

Mom shook her head. "Not really. Your father's been getting very upsetting reports. Those cousins took Russell only because they thought they could make some money out of it. Russell was giving them nearly all of what he was earning on his grocery-delivery job, and your father was sending something extra every week. But the cousins kept asking for more and cutting corners on Russell's meals and clean linen. Your father never suggested it, but I realized I should offer to let his only brother move in here with us. And Russell's really a sweet, gentle person, Ollie. You'll like him, I promise."

"So what about your college courses?" I asked. We were back to that again. Mom had been hanging on despite the growing work load, going to class three nights a week and cramming in as much reading and studying as she could the rest of the time. She'd been looking more tired than ever lately, and kind of sad too, going off to school in the evenings in her droopy jeans and an old fringed jacket of Merrie's.

Mom sighed. "I'm giving up college, Ollie. I've done a lot of thinking about it these past weeks. And first things come first. I have to do what I feel is

175

right for me. I can't let other people's ideas shape my life."

I was stunned and also very happy. But I tried hard not to show it. I didn't want Mom to think I was gloating.

"You're not doing this because . . . because of me," I stammered, "because of the things I said about your paying more attention to Meredith's ideas than to mine?"

Mom put her arms around me. "No, Ollie. I just told you. This is my own idea. We each have our own tastes and abilities. I'm most comfortable doing 'homebody' type things for my family, as long as I'm needed at that kind of job. Adding on school meant spreading myself awfully thin. I guess I could have gone on managing it though with some strain, except for Uncle Russell's coming. That forced me to come to a point of decision. So, in a way, I'm kind of glad it happened."

"I understand," I said, hugging her back with relief. "I really do. Miss Kilhenny wouldn't approve of it, though."

Mom smiled. "Miss Kilhenny isn't really involved in this, is she?"

I pulled away from Mom suddenly. "What about Merrie?" I asked darkly. "Won't she just have fits when you tell her that Uncle Russell's moving in and you're quitting school?"

"I've already told her," Mom replied quietly. "I felt I owed her that. She was very sincere about wanting me to go to college, Ollie. She wanted the best for me. *Her* idea of the best, though."

"So how'd she take it? That and . . . and the other news?"

Mom raised her hands and dropped them. "She's pouting, of course. But she'll get over it. I told her that the way she accepted *both* pieces of news would be a test of her maturity. Because it's time for Meredith to grow up. She's old enough and she's smart enough."

It's all fixed already for Uncle Russell to work at Pop's gas station. That'll be the second new person he'll have given a job to in the last couple of weeks. Norman Delaney finally had his hearing before the judge and, after he promised to make a truly fresh start in life and Pop offered him a training job in the repair shop at the service station, he was released into his mother's custody. Mrs. Delaney says Pop is "a blessed soul and a dear saint." Harvey Epping also had his hearing and now he seems to have vanished for good. Maybe the judge knows where he is, but if he does he isn't saying.

On the way home from school today, I told Anita about my Uncle Russell coming to live with us after all.

She nodded. "I hope it works out okay," she said. "I'm sure it will. I have news, too," she added, a little out of breath. "You'll never guess who's getting married. At Christmas time."

I thought a minute. "Well, offhand I'd say you and Hughie Rand. But I don't think you could. Not even in the South Sea islands."

"Oh, Olivia!" Anita blushed. "You're terrible, really. We're only going steady. Sort of." She knew I didn't exactly approve. Even though Stevie had given me that hand-carved olive-wood necklace, he and I were still only friends. It was different.

"Now think," Anita demanded. "She's a relative of mine."

My mind skipped quickly over Grandma Castellani and little Aunt Helen. "Your Aunt Bea," I said easily. "Who to?"

"You know him," Anita answered, almost irritably.

"I do?" I couldn't think of any single man. Heaven help me, not my Mr. Jenner. I wasn't ready to share him with Anita's Aunt Bea. Not with anybody. Not yet.

"Think hard," Anita urged. "He spoke to us that time when I took you to the Beauty Boo-Teek."

"The Beauty Boo . . . Oh, *that* guy."

Anita's expression grew serious. "Why do you say it that way?"

"What way?"

" '*That* guy.' Perry's nice," she added defensively. "Don't you think so? Handsome, lots of laughs. Besides, he's got a part ownership in the Boo-Teek, too. So, if they get married, his twenty-five percent and my Aunt Bea's thirty percent make fifty-five percent, and that gives them a controlling interest."

"Oh, I see," I said slowly. "Why do they have to get married, though? Why can't they just become business partners?"

"Gee, I never thought of that," Anita remarked. "Why couldn't they? That way maybe I'd still have a chance at the Boo-Teek."

"What do you mean 'a chance'? I thought it was all set that your Aunt Bea was going to teach you the business and give you a job there."

"Yes, I know," Anita admitted, tapping her foot and looking down at the toe of her shoe. We had reached the front walk of her house. "But, you see, Perry's got lots of ideas. He thinks he and Bea should sell their controlling interest in it and open a new place in a richer neighborhood. I'm not sure I'd fit into those plans."

Anita threw back her head and fluffed out her hair with one hand. "Well, I don't care really. It is kind of romantic, their getting married. And I wish them luck. But, as for me, working in a beauty shop probably wouldn't be all that great. Hair all over the place and cranky customers either griping about their troubles or showing off. I walked Hughie past there last Saturday and asked him if he wanted to go inside. He said definitely *no* and what did *I* ever want with a beauty shop. He said that one of the reasons he likes me so much is that everything I have is real and honest and natural. Nothing artificial."

Anita raised her eyes to mine and bit her lower lip until it was white. Her cheeks were burning.

I was too overcome to tease her about it.

"I'm glad," I said, "that he . . . he thinks so much of you. It shows Hughie has a lot of sense after all. So, as long as you might not be going to work in the beauty shop, it probably wouldn't hurt you to stay in school a little longer and take up something that would get you a better job. You might even get to like school after a while."

Anita shifted her books to her other arm. "Oh, school's okay. Kilhenny doesn't bother me very much. In fact, the whole class says she's been a lot easier on everybody since you left. So, like you say, maybe I won't be quitting when I'm sixteen. But," she touched my arm shyly, "I know one thing. I'll never be a brain like you, Olivia."

"Like me?" I exclaimed, astonished. "Why like me? Why'd you say that, Anita?"

She hunched her shoulders. "Because . . . you're not just 'ordinary' smart. You're smart in a special way. It's the way you figure things out, I guess—like the way you figured out that Norman Delaney stole his own mother's television set. And then you even proved it. Just like a real, honest-to-goodness TV detective. I was talking to my mother and grandmother about that just the other day. They said it'll probably turn out that you're some kind of a genius."

I began to laugh disbelievingly. "A genius, me, Olivia Potts?"

Anita nodded. "Yeah, really. And I agreed they were right. I think you're a genius, too."

"Oh," I started to say, "that's the dumbest . . ." But I stopped before the word came out. Because I remembered that Anita wasn't really dumb at all. In fact, in her own way, she was actually pretty smart.

The MS READ-a-thon needs young readers!

Boys and girls between 6 and 14 can join the MS READ-a-thon and help find a cure for Multiple Sclerosis by reading books. And they get two rewards — the enjoyment of reading, and the great feeling that comes from helping others.

Parents and educators: For complete information call your local MS chapter, or call toll-free (800) 243-6000. Or mail the coupon below.

Kids can help, too!